Grimes' Punishment

A

Blood, Sex and Brawls

Novel

Written by

H.A.L. Wagner

Edited by

James Troy

Published by

FORKER MEDIA

Grimes' Punishment A Blood, Sex and Brawls Novel © 2017 H.A.L. WAGNER

ISBN: 9781942657057

For more information: www.forkermedia.com

Email: forkermedia@gmail.com

For Mark,

This is what we wanted even if it isn't how we wanted it to go...

...we'll get there one day.

The Grimes Collection:

Grimes' Punishment A Blood, Sex and Brawls Novel

Grimes' Retribution A Debt Paid in Full Novel

Grimes' Reckoning A Waking the Dead Novel

Grimes' Redux You Only Die Twice Novel

Thank you for reading Grimes' Punishment. This is the first of four novels in the Grimes series. Grimes is a unique character, an anti-hero that he didn't want to become. These stories take place in and around Daytona Beach, Florida. If you live in the area, or vacation there, you may recognize the streets, buildings, and sandy beaches. As with many stories, I have changed or exaggerated a few things, so this is not an exact match for the city. Enjoy.

Thanks,

HW

Instagram: @hal_writes

Contents

Baptism

It was an old oak, the wide trunk ascended into thick and twisted limbs struggling against age and gravity to reach the sky. A thick limb with nobs of sawn-off branches hung over the wooden privacy fence. I hoisted myself up, grabbing hold of the thick chunks of bark and scooted along the limb of the tree. It gave me the perfect vantage to watch Daniel Watson, forty-two-year-old Daytona Beach resident clean his gutters. Watson was in the process of suing his employer because of a work-related injury. The employer claimed he could no longer do what was required for his job. So, the employer hired the law firm of Willis Sanford P.A., then Willis hired me. My first job as a licensed private investigator. After two days of following Daniel Watson, I was in a position to capture him in his lie.

I took out a small video recorder and pressed the red button. The limb, narrow where I now stood, bounced with every breath but I got a clear shot of Watson in full motion removing clumps of pine needles from the gutter. His butt crack extended beyond his waistband as he struggled to get the far corners of the gutters. *This was easy and even fun.* I inched further and further from the trunk of the grand oak. The branch began to wobble, forcing me to drop the camera and claw for the trunk. Below was the yard and beyond that, Watson. The supposedly handicapped man turned with ease to see me wobbling as the bend and sway of the extending branch was too much on this private investigator's inner ear. I lost my battle with gravity, the ground jumped up at me, I dropped into the man's yard.

I tasted turf as I scrambled to my feet, leaving the camera recording. Watson rushed down the ladder, leaning forward to offer his assistance until he spotted the camera. He straightened up, took a deep breath, and yelled, "Get the hell outta my yard you piece of shit!" Snot blew from his nostrils as he stomped his feet. He charged hard like a rhino.

I was on my feet now but chose to remain low in stance. Watson tossed a forward jetting leg. Grabbing hold of the ankle I twisted. The man went the way of his foot as it rotated, spinning him over and to the ground. Watson lay stunned for a second then dug his fingers into the sod as he pushed himself up.

Anger built in my veins. I wanted to lunge forward and attack, but my training countered what I had always known. The P.I. is not to be seen or interacted with, my life wasn't some pulp novel filled with blood, sex, and brawls. I had the pictures and video proof that Watson was faking an injury, and a much-needed paycheck would soon follow. Everything was going in my favor until I spotted the glint of a blade in the bright yellow sun.

A quick sidestep got me out of the first attack, then a swift pull back as Watson swung the four-inch blade around. Watson left his arm wide, I stepped in, grabbed his wrist, and twisted. The man let out a yelp and dropped the blade. I kicked his knee, sending him back to the ground where he lay breathing heavily but otherwise not moving. The fight was gone.

I stood fully upright and lowered my hands. I checked my camera, saw it working, and smiled at Watson, "Busted." I said and sprinted off to the fence, scaling it with ease.

Once back in my truck I looked at the Watson homestead. The man, red faced, was peering over the fence and shouting. I laughed and sped away.

As the Florida sun descended, a burnt orange hue settled over everything, I felt a soft whirl beginning within my gut. I fought a smile as the sense of accomplishment flushed my cheeks and increased the depth to my smiling crow's feet.

My first job as a private detective was complete. The waiting was over, the seal popped, now with one job complete I was ready to take on more. The video evidence was in the camera and soon would be in my client's hands and money would soon be in mine. Of all the things I had gambled on in my life, choosing me was the best bet. The last of my cash was spent on a license and an internet ad. Today's job got me to break even and I can only go up from here.

There had been days in my life I was proud of, and times I could not help but smile, like the time I cracked a gun safe with a "B" burglary rating. The safe had a combination lock that took a lot of practice and a lot of patience to open, but when that heavy steel door squealed open the same sense of accomplishment, I felt today melted all over my body. Those safecracking days are gone for good. I have a new way to feel satisfied.

I drove along, my mind jumping from memory to memory of the thieving days. The days of large scores with my best friend and criminal mentor, Billy Horseblood. Billy and I had a good run after I got the boot from boot camp, I didn't belong in that man's Army. Conformity wasn't becoming. Freedom meant hitting banks, boosting cars, and smashing jewelry stores, never clocking in or out. Vacation requests meant how long the money lasted between jobs. Things were starting to work out for me. I had cash, I had the perception of freedom with the world for the taking. It was a great way to spend my twenties.

The last bank job we pulled went like clockwork, very routine. We picked a bank that sat at the front of a shopping plaza and near two intersecting highways. One minute after two and I got the drop on the guard, removed his gun, and put him on the floor. All the tellers were well rehearsed in their bank training, I was in control. My latex gloved hand was steady holding the gun on the tellers as I went down the line. Their stacks of cash dropped in the bag, filling it for a good take. My mask was on, my wig was straight, clockwork.

Through the sun and the glass, I saw the stolen Dodge Charger pull up with Billy behind the wheel. He had on his floppy hat and sunglasses. I knew his knee was bouncing, keeping his foot off the gas. The rear window was down, ready for my swan dive and then he would slap that skinny peddle. It's why we preferred sedans. My blood was pumping as much as his. We were at the top of our bank robbing game. Then I turned and locked eyes with her.

The mother clutched her daughter tight, her own face buried away, refusing to look at me. She probably watched crime stories convincing her if she didn't look at me, if she never saw my face, she would be safe. Her daughter, a fair-haired cherub girl with soft brown eyes, hadn't heard that before. She was looking at me, right through my mask and into what was left of my soul. Her watery browns formed pikes that stabbed into my chest. Her chin tucked and crinkled as her lip quivered. She began to shake as her mom squeezed her tighter, begging her to be quiet, assuring her it would be over soon.

Training, or instinct, whatever you want to call it had me on auto pilot and the pistol was trained on her before my eyes ever focused showing my brain what I was looking at. Had she moved, I'd have shot her before I could tell my finger not to.

My stomach dropped and I tucked my head and ran for the door. The girl's stare rocked me inside, knocking me off my game. Otherwise, I would have seen the guard pull his backup piece. He fired twice. The first bullet shattered the glass door. The other punched me square in the back. I managed to stay on my feet.

We sped off leaving the bank in our dust, but I couldn't leave the image of that girl.

The vest I had on stopped the three-eighty round, but not the pain. I never told Billy. He celebrated our take in the usual fashion of alcohol and drugs in the company of people we should never have associated with. I went along with it carrying a stomach full of rocks as that little girl looped in my head. It didn't matter the amount of alcohol; nothing washed it away. So, when we were out of cash once more and it was time to start casing a bank, I told Billy no.

Billy shrugged, "Okay brother, ain't no big thing." That's how it went.

Together we did well over the years, most importantly we got away clean. My bank robbing days were done, but my life as a thief carrying on.

Chapter 1

She tugged on her blond ponytail, synching it tight and said, "Your key fits my lock, so you can let yourself in anytime, Grimes."

I sat on the most uncomfortable couch imaginable. The red and brown woven fiber pattern scraped like burlap on my skin and wooden arms put an ache on my elbow. My duplex had drab light grey walls and white tile throughout, something that is easy to get the sand out when you live beachside. It was 11 am and I had not put pants on today or yesterday. In fact, I was going on three days without having the need to put pants on at all. Three weeks went by, and the lawyer hadn't called with any new jobs. I checked my email and there was nothing in there either. The high of working for a living was quickly fading.

My phone lit with an unfamiliar number.

"Hello." I said, still had not put to memory a proper *Grimes Investigations* greeting yet.

"Yo, brother." Billy exhaled nicotine infused smoke, "How's work?" he rasped on the other end.

"Nonexistent. I haven't moved from my chair in three days."

"Smitty called." Billy let the words hang. Discussing Smitty was the reason I didn't recognize the phone number. Business like this was reserved for burner phones. "He wants us back for another job."

"Not interested." I lied; I needed the money. All that cash I had taken in over the years passed through my hands as fast as I made it. There were a few investments I made to help friends. I owned a third of Billy's automotive shop and half of Ben Saadon's MMA School. Ben was former Mossad and had trained me in mixed martial arts when I was young. I also owned half of a bicycle shop. The bike shop was started by a pretty brunette I dated. It seemed like a good idea at the time, but she peddled away and so did my money.

"I know *you're out.*" Billy said it like it was a bad thing. "I had to run it by you. Ever since that trouble with the IRS, I've been doing everything right at the shop, which means I'm not making much money." Billy sucked in on his cigarette.

"I'm trying to be good here," I said. Billy knew what I meant.

"Will you just meet with him? Smitty took to your new line of work pretty well considering how things were handled back in his day. Besides we kinda owe him."

"We don't owe Smitty shit." Telling Smitty I was out, took more courage, but it had to end sometime; it was going to end somehow, but not yet.

"You can tell it to his face tomorrow." Billy said then hung up. It wasn't like him at all to be so uptight about a job or anything. Smitty brought the pressure. Smitty, just Smitty, no first name and no last. He ran the numbers in town and became our fence. The mob had moved out of Daytona years ago, Smitty was the hangover, the last Goodfella. The mob ran gambling and prostitution for decades. By the 1960's most of it dried up. Back then,

Smitty was just a kid running messages and errands for bosses with names that carried their own entourage of FBI. He got pinched, never said a word, and when he got out, he just hung around the dog track all day everyday as a bookie but always had a wad of cash on him. You could always spot him, white hair, a gold tooth, and a scar under his left eye that said he saw too much.

One day he came to us with a plan to elevate our game beyond hitting banks and stealing cars. Smitty took us in and showed us how to hit bigger targets, places after hours, places without crying children. At twenty I was eager to grow my career.

Together, we took being thieves seriously. Smitty paid for me to get locksmith training. My house quickly filled with every kind of lock, both electrical and mechanical, possible. Smitty enrolled us in several corporate security training courses from a variety of companies. *Keep your enemies close.* We learned everything they knew, surveillance, guard training, firearms training, and driving, though Billy was one of the best drivers I ever saw. Then we knew what they knew, and it made getting in and out so much easier.

The groundwork was being laid to move us off the street and into bigger and bolder heists. Things like art and precious metals. Living the dream alright but the reality was Smitty was old and living in the past. There wasn't much work out there for the hard steal.

Then I got pinched.

The Daytona cops had Billy and me in their sites since I was in high school. Nothing would stick to us because we never pulled a job in Volusia County, you don't shit where you eat. I was labeled 'known associates' with a lot of the criminal underbelly of this town, which did me in. We had hit a jewelry store up north and came back to get rid of anything that tied us to it, including our tools. I usually bought my tools off a couple of Mexican guys and never asked where they came from. We would buy and sell often in the used tool market, always in cash and never from a store. I had a battery powered drill and several batteries along with some other junk listed at a yard sale. PD was all over me. They came prepared with a list of tools from a recent pawn store heist I had nothing to do with.

One thing led to another, and I refused to explain where I got them, so I got it hard. Since it was under $500, I got charged with a misdemeanor but got the book thrown at me. The judge had seen me walk a couple of times, but not this time. I was locked up for nine months.

It all seemed so glamorous, the cash the hush-hush of I what I really did for a living. I felt like a spy and tried to live like they do in the movies. Truthfully, I was a dirt bag, a common thief who didn't want to get a real job. It wasn't a victimless crime, I learned that sitting in my cell for nine months fighting off ass grabbers and neo-Nazis pissed I wouldn't join. All I thought about were the old people clinging to their social security checks, and the kids waiting for a lollypop only to be confronted with my Glock in their face. I had to make a serious change, I had to make amends for the fear I cast on the innocent. I know the day is coming, the day I get what I deserve. When it comes, I want it to be a better one, not for me but for those around me.

After I got out, I told Billy I was done with all of it. I didn't want to steal anymore cars, rob banks, or participate in any corporate heists. I hated prison enough to know that I never would go back. I knew I didn't want to turn wrenches at Billy's shop either, so I took a career skills test, and it listed private investigator. Telling Smitty I was out, took more courage, but it had to end sometime; it was going to end somehow, but according to Billy, not yet.

Those days living on the edge were great times but the weight on me was too much to bare. This new bubbling of emotion was something different, this new gig as a private investigator meant something. Making a few hundred dollars for three days of work was chump-change compared to a bank job making $7,200 in two and a half minutes. The job wasn't over. I had to check the video and turn them over to the lawyer, Sanford. It wasn't the work alone, or completing the assignment, which was making me happy. It was the combination of hard work and a paycheck, together, that made me legitimate, nearly honest, and I did it all on my own. I pulled a job legally and now could be paid, legally. I would have to start paying taxes and change my status with the IRS from freelancer to private investigator. From a life of crime, this meant something, something new.

None of that mattered now, the money was gone replaced with bills stacked high on the coffee table. Billy's shop wasn't making money so every month I tell him to roll any profits he tries to pay me back into the business. The same thing with Ben. He had a fighter he wanted to turn pro, that cost money. One day I can cash in all this generosity or die a sucker. I had to make this investigation business work by any means.

A knock at the door got me off the couch. I didn't bother with pants; in fact, it didn't even occur to me. At the door was Chloe, the smoking hot 37-year-old mother of one blond boy named Tab. Chloe owned the duplex I rented half of. She lived next door and would often knock the rent down if I watched her kid or fixed things. The boy was nine and didn't need much supervision other than a PlayStation. I was not up to baby sit today.

"Hi, Roger." Chloe wore a big smile full of prescription whitened teeth. She was tall with a fit body that came from four days a week in the gym and a set of store-bought tits.

Her job as a real-estate agent perfected that salesman smile, convincing me I made the right decision on whatever she was selling. Her bottle blond streaked hair was pulled back into a ponytail, and she had on a tight tank top and yoga pants that matched. Today must be one of those gym days.

"Hi." I was never much for words. In fact, I hate talking. I'm waiting for the day we can all just communicate telepathically.

She took her time replying as her golden-brown eyes went up and down, scanning over my own fit body. We went to the same gym, it's how we met, and I started living next door. She had tried several times to hook up, but I never let it get that far and she hasn't quit. I had become particular with the women I let into my world. Lessons learned over the years left me with major trust issues. I would rather stay single then be holed up in the slammer because some broad liked to brag to her friends about how I made my money. Maybe that can change now that I 've quit stealing for a living.

"Hey, is that a new tattoo?" She looked over my tatted shoulders covering most of the flesh down to both elbows. Her chit chat would get her nowhere.

I shook my head, "Nope." A salty ocean breeze rolled through and suddenly I became aware I was standing in my boxers.

I watched her eyes travel from my mid-section to meet my eyes. She smiled showing a little of her tongue pushing at the backs of her teeth. Her eyes danced with the things she wanted from me.

"I didn't think guys wore boxers anymore, just those boxer briefs." Her neck stretched out peering around the door. There was no denying the raw sexuality oozing from every pour. Lean muscle rounded out each arm, only her midsection held the smallest of pooch signaling deep in my brain she was fertile triggering a latent caveman instinct to spread my genes and make more of me. *Not now*, I told myself, beating the caveman into submission.

My silence got her talking again, "So I wanted to ask you," Chloe ran a hand over her ponytail and gave it a little tug, I felt the breeze on my shorts once more. My brow protruded; my beard thickened as my shoulders hunched. I wanted to grab a spear and kill a mammoth for her. A hard, dry, swallow and I evolved.

"If I gave you a key, could you let Tab in and make sure he gets settled? He has early release at one and I have a showing at twelve-thirty." She let the favor hang there. She was always in a pinch except when there was something she really wanted to do. It's one of the things I did not like about her.

"I'll be here, unless I get a case." I didn't mind watching the kid, but it was becoming an ever-increasing task. My shoulder was not one I wanted her to lean on.

"I think he's getting old enough to be home alone." Her golden-brown eyes locked me down. She finally broke the gaze, reached into her purse, and pulled a shiny newly cut brass key, still with the burrs from milling. "Here. If you could let him in and maybe get him a drink and a snack, I'm sure he would be okay." She put the key in my opened palm. "I'll be back by two at the latest."

I knew she wouldn't be. It would be more like four because something would inevitably come up that she had to attend to instead of her kid.

"Okay." I took the key. I thought the conversation was over, but I heard her take a breath.

"I haven't seen you at the gym lately."

"Yeah." I said, leaving the word hanging there without any more to say. I had not been to the gym in a while. I ran a hand over my shaved head, feeling the tiny hairs like a bristle brush against my palm.

"Let me know sometime if you want to. I'm flexible." Chloe smiled at her own pun and walked off knowing I was watching her go. She turned catching me watching her and said, "And you can keep that key."

She watched me from her car for a few seconds and I swear she licked her lips. I shut the door upset with myself for not being firmer about not watching her kid.

The next night I was sitting up in bed; just a sheet covered my nude body. It was another hot night in Daytona Beach and funds had run out along with the patience of the electric company. I knew it was coming and when it did, I took a cold shower before bed and again in the middle of the night to take care of the night sweats.

After the second shower, I sat in the dark with the widows open, listening to the rhythmic whooshing of the waves curling in on the beach. Judging by the sound they were small tight curls. I hadn't surfed all summer, mostly because the ocean resembled a lake. Soon hurricane season would pick up and bring the swells back.

Staring at the black mirror of my cell, I knew it had about thirty five percent charge left. I didn't want to waste it mindless videos or news articles that were anything but news.

Cars drifted along A1A, some exhausts throaty and deep from v8 performance, others light and soft from four cylinders. Three am came and went as I watched my cell phone light up the dark room. I had it on silent because falling asleep in the humid night air was hard enough without any interruptions. I let the light shine until it was black again, there was no hurry to check the number, it had to be Billy. I blew off the meeting with him and Smitty.

I knew the kind of job Smitty wanted to set up. Something that would take planning and involving more players. People would need to be paid off and the information had to be right. All too fast it would become a daily job, more like going to the office than robbing a jewelry store. I would rather be breaking than controlled. Some days I was glad I got tossed in jail just to get out of the cycle I was in.

Now I was on my own, unable to pay the electric bill and sitting in the heat of the night. As I argued with myself over whether it was justifiable for a starving man stealing bread to survive, the caller left a message.

The call passed to voicemail and so did another heist for a lot of money. I was mad at myself but knew if I were to answer it would lead to a meeting, then a plan and then a heist. I would hate myself even more. So, with all that worked out in my head, I got up and got a cold beer from the fridge courtesy the hot mom who lived next door and her long extension cord.

The cold beer was a relief and I wanted to thank Chloe in the flesh, but it felt too cheap to throw her a bone even though it was all she wanted in return. I was just not that kind of guy. Women, more specifically getting laid, were not a top priority for me. Judging by the phone numbers and forward conversations from women while just trying to enjoy a pint at the bar was testament to my good looks. At 6'2" with a lean muscular build and two half sleeves of tattoos, I had a healthy self-esteem which is why I never pursued women. Nothing good had ever come from any of my past relationships with my past profession being what it was. I hung my P.I. shingle, the decision was made to lay off the women, at least until I can pay my bills.

The ultimate lesson about women came one night while heading back up to the bar after taking a piss. There she sat, Christine or Christy or whatever her name, she was talking to a woman next to her and they seemed to be getting along. Crystal's elbows were increasingly baring the load of her head as it neared the bar. As I approached to claim my barstool, I heard her say it, "Yeah well, my boyfriend is a thief, like not just cars but like safe cracker. It's all he does, sits in his living room and takes safes apart."

The new friend, just as drunk, didn't believe her or would not even remember the claim, but that was not the point. I had let one in too far. This girl had seen it all and worse was proven to not be able to keep her mouth shut. So, without ever taking that seat, I walked out.

The next day I was down at the tattoo parlor. A World War Two style battleship was sinking into the backside of my bicep with the words, *Loose Lips*.

Here I was in the dark sitting on a sticky imitation leather recliner letting the salty breeze come in through the east facing window. Sweating in the midnight humidity was not working for me, curiosity got the best of me, and I checked the message on my phone. It was Willis Sanford, he apologized for the late call not realizing it was the middle of the night. I must admit the man worked for the money. The message went on with an invite up to the seventh floor in the morning with no other explanation.

The call was perfect timing, I needed another job. My mind was already spending the next fifteen hundred eggs before they were hatched in my account. The heat was driving me madder than the boredom of not working. Newly $1,500 deposit into my account would be another fresh start. Living beachside was nice but it was time to get out, time to get an office and get set up for business. Or I could call Smitty and pull a job I didn't want.

I finally fell asleep tasting the food and drink I would treat myself to after my meeting with Mr. Sanford.

When the sun came up it brought the heat. I was stuck to the brown pleather chair and for a moment thought my skin would peel right off as I sat up. My front door was open, but the screen door closed. I sat on the edge of the chair staring out at the glistening dew on the grass. Outside somewhere a seagull screamed, and I heard the loud pipes of a Harley race up A1A. With the A/C off and already sweating, I looked at the floor and decided to skip my morning routine of core exercises. I hated myself but opted out anyway.

Standing with the refrigerator door open, the cold dry air blocked out all thoughts as I enjoyed the relief. The compressor kicked me out of my trance. It was still early, but the heat was already climbing. Meeting with Willis meant air conditioning. There was no real reason Willis would be at his office this early after a three am phone call but waiting there was better than here.

I put on a pair of dark blue Dickie's, a black pocket t-shirt and a pair of Vans slip-ons and left.

Driving towards Sanford's office, he looked down at me from his billboard. I guessed his age just north of sixty with black tight curled hair that shaped uniformly around his head. A small patch of white, like a little cotton ball was intruding around the widow's peak. He had a big smile and steel rim glasses over deep brown eyes. I hoped he had a case for me. The first one came, and I ate and drank happily for a week. Then nothing. It felt like a tease, like all show and no go.

Sanford's office was the tallest building for blocks. The beige-colored building stood just off the corner of International Speedway and South Ridgewood. Down the center of the six stories were shiny mirrored glass windows wrapped in bright chrome trim creating a diamond pattern with the letters CBR across it, I didn't know what CBR meant and didn't care. Mist from a small star-shaped fountain covered my face as I entered the building.

Off the elevator, I made a left and went into Willis's office. There was a small waiting area with stiff looking red and beige chairs pushed against beige walls. Hanging in the middle was a zebra skin crossed by Zulu warriors' spears. A small oval shaped table had magazines of varying titles, mostly to do with law and insurance. One had Willis's face on the cover, a big white toothy smile, his arms folded, he had on a blue pinstriped suit and was leaning against that immovable desk of his.

The reception desk to the left of the main office door was empty. The chair was pushed out and a purse occupied the seat. I decided not to knock and grabbed the door handle.

The place was a huge corner office on the seventh floor with windows covering two of the five walls. From here, on a clear day Willis Sanford could see the river and the beach beyond that. A black marble countertop covered a well-stocked bar with brands that I had never tasted. His desk was a heavy cherry wood that sank into the plush grey carpet with the permanence of a war monument. On the other wall were two large bookcases filled with mostly law books, but I caught a few history and art titles.

Inside, Sanford was seated at his desk. A face I recognized from the billboards looked back at me. His deep brown eyes were wrapped in square metal framed glasses, his jacket was off and so was his tie. His crisp white shirt had the top two buttons undone. The white under shirt contrasted against his dark skin. Both sleeves were rolled up and, in his hands, he held a breakfast sandwich from a drive-thru up the street. Those gleaming white teeth of his were sinking in mid-bite as I entered.

A young woman sat in one of two dark brown leather chairs across from the huge desk. Her black hair was straight and pulled tight against her head the excess was wrapped in a bun in the back. She wore purple slacks and a sheer white blouse. Overall, very nice to look at. In front of her was an unwrapped sandwich of her own waiting until she finished sipping a cup of coffee very carefully, desperately avoiding a scolded mouth. Her eyes met mine as mine left Sanford's.

"Sorry to barge in." I said, looking at them both as they devoured the fast food. I stood without coming any further into the office.

Sanford swallowed his bite and waved me over while he wiped the corner of his mouth with a paper napkin. "Come on in. Have a seat, Roger." His words came out fast with short pauses like a bubble maker, words flew out and hovered there while my brain caught up to everything he was saying.

I nodded and then nodded to the receptionist before taking my seat. We sat in silence except for the chewing and swallowing sound both made until the receptionist's sandwich was done and she then collected all the trash and left. I wasn't sure what to make of her silence, nothing seemed to be going on, not even a conversation, before I came in. I had not met her the first time I was in the office and a lack of a formal introduction made me feel out of place.

Sanford brushed his hands together and then held his palms out like a magician convincing you there was nothing up his sleeve. He took a sip of coffee that was not nearly as hot as it had been when I came in. On the desk was a gold wristwatch and platinum diamond pinky ring. He clasped the watch and slipped on the ring then stood. The diamond looked to be three carats and a little cloudy and yellow, a nice stone.

"Monique brought me breakfast. We typically start our day with something to eat and chat about this and that." Sanford spit the words out with a pause between sentences. Seeing him in person instead of a billboard revealed he was of average height around 5'10" and was on the thin side. He wore his gray slacks high and opted for suspenders that were hanging loose on either side now.

Sanford pushed up on the bridge of his glasses before speaking once more, "That was some fast work you did on the Watson case." He talked more with his hands than his mouth as they danced back and forth, open palms with widespread fingers jutting out and coming back quickly like a shadow boxer warming up. "Yes sir, not bad for a newbie."

The bounce in his step, the way his feet never crossed, there was no doubt in my mind he used to be a fighter and it made me relaxed, like I knew the guy already. I bet there was a time when he was good. They said I was good, back at Ben's MMA school, really good. He wanted to sponsor me, turn me pro one day. Billy talked me out of it, convincing me I didn't want to get punched in the head my whole life. Most days it still feels like I am. Sanford danced on, talking about the case I closed and what happened to Watson and so on. It didn't really concern me. That money was spent, and I needed more. Finally, he got to the point.

"I wanna snatch you up Grimes before the other law offices in town find out how good you are, if you really are that good or just lucky." Sanford said as he moved around to my side of the desk. He snagged at his pant leg, lifting the cuff over his ankle as his leg came to rest on the corner of the desk.

Sanford stared at me for a few seconds, "You don't talk much." He stated with zero inflection of a question. "Fine. I can always do all the talking. So, retainer then?" that time he was asking.

I nodded without words. He went back around to his side of the desk and sat back in his chair. A cushion of air whistled out as he settled into the soft maroon leather. His fingers drummed on the large cherry wood desk. Then they danced over to his computer and started typing.

"I can email a contract." I said finally, pulling my cell.

Sanford smirked, "First thing you got to learn about working with lawyers is we ain't never gonna sign a contract we didn't draft. Not with a PI anyway." He didn't look up from his computer. "How's twenty-five hundred a month plus three hundred dollars at the start of every case for expenses and seventy-five an hour billable?" This time he asked a question that was more of a statement. I couldn't say no to a raise, so I nodded my acceptance. Then he told me he needed me to say it, so I did. Snappy fingers punched at the keyboard while I stared out the window. Sanford held his head up with his eyes pressing down through the lenses of the large glasses as he typed. Then I heard a ding on my cell and there was a new email. The first payment went through.

Sanford stood up and went to his wet bar. He picked up a bottle of Remy Martin and looked back at me with raised eyebrows. I shook my head no, and he poured three fingers into the glass. Next, he reached below to a mini fridge and pulled out a small bottle of champagne and filled the rest of the glass with it. He took a sip and let out his breath then did a little James Brown styled dance, "This is a good way to start your day right here."

With a hop, Sanford made his way over to the large window and looked out at the famous beach town below bathed in golden Florida sun. "I grew up here. Right over there actually." He pressed a finger against the glass towards the west. Though I couldn't make out what house he was talking about I knew the neighborhood. It was near Bethune-Cookman College, and I knew it had always been an African American neighborhood since before segregation.

"When I was a kid, we had our own beach. We, I mean us black folks." His words slowed and his hands weren't dancing. "How *rich* we were." He smiled, it faded quickly. "Finally, back before you were born, we all integrated. A lot of things changed in this town over the years except that neighborhood. It ain't changed much."

Sanford turned back to me. "I don't tell you all this to cast white guilt or any of that bullshit. I'm just saying I've been here my whole life. Yeah, used to train at a gym called Pouncey's, right over there. Lightweight I was. My momma wouldn't have me fighting so I went off to Stetson, a poor boy and came back a lawyer. I worked hard and fought with my brain instead of my hands after that. Now I'm up here with a big corner office. I mingle with the wealthy, with folks that would never pass through my neighborhood, not now and not then."

His steps back around to his desk lacked bounce. His hands went up on the desk and he spread his long fingers out. His dark roast-colored eyes were on me. Webs of red veins covered the whites of his eyes. "There's an infestation down there in that neighborhood. Rats, that what they got there, rats." Sanford's eyes glazed over, and his breath got heavy. His mind went someplace he didn't want to go, someplace he wanted to take me but was not finding the words that would lead me there.

I knew what that was like, wandering, getting lost in your own thoughts and memories and how you would change things to make them happier. It was futile and the longer you lingered there the more vivid your mistakes and the life you could have had ways you down. Each time you're there, the tougher it is to snap back.

"Sir," I said.

"I know you Grimes," Sanford's lower lip protruded. He stood again and sipped his Remi, "Not this fella' you trying to change into."

My palms went all wet, but I kept my cool as I had the hundred times cops hauled me in.

"Like I told you, I come from over there and now I'm up here. You can too, Grimes, but them Rats." His head dropped as it rocked side to side, "Them rats need exterminating. That's why I picked you, a thief and common criminal pulling off this fantastic con of being a strait-laced private investigator."

I felt the blood depleting from my face; I must have been an ashy white because suddenly a smile broke across Sanford's face. "Aw Mr. Grimes," The brightness with an edge came back to his eyes. "I'm looking forward to working with you." He finished the last of his drink then said, "Well I guess that's it."

I wasn't sure what to say or do. Sanford's reason for outing me as a criminal baffled me. I stood slowly, turned, and found my way out.

The receptionist was at her desk. I saw on her monitor there was an Amazon webpage up, she was looking at shoes, gold heels to be exact.

"Welcome to the club," she said without looking up at me from her shoe shopping. With a grin, I moved on, out the door and down the six flights to the hot outdoors.

Chapter 2

"Roger, man don't do this." Pope's eyes were deep brown; the crease above his brow intensified with his words. "We've got two weeks of basic left. It's not worth it." The night was black and out there past the gate it was even blacker.

I ran into the darkness chasing a score and fulfill the urges deep within me. I felt terrible for it. Pope wanted a career, I wanted out.

Two days after my new retainer deposited, I signed the lease on an office on the second floor of a building in the downtown area on Beach Street. Chloe helped me find it ensuring she will be hanging around. The new office was nice, a river view and an Irish Pub a block down that didn't already know me. The office had a small kitchenette with sink and small fridge. The bathroom was down the hall but best of all the electric was part of the lease, so the A/C stayed on all the time. With a couch moved in and a desk I found in the trash everything was ready to go.

With most of my money spent I sat at my desk wondering what to do next. It was early, about 9 am and I wanted to get this day started. I skimmed some social media, read a few news articles, and did my push-ups and sit-ups. It was now 9:45 am.

The cellphone dinged indicating a new email. I grabbed the tablet and checked the inbox. There was an email forwarded from Willis. There was no message in the body of the email, just the original email.

The email went as follows:

Mr. Grimes,

I need your help in locating my daughter, Milo. The girl has run away from home. Before you give me a canned response about calling the cops or give it time, there are some very specific circumstances that have caused her to run. My wife passed when Milo was only ten. That's when it all changed for Milo. She began to skip school and spend the weekends at friends' houses. Now she is gone.

Willis thinks you can help. I don't know what to do and the police aren't helping.

Thanks,

Gregg Hines

(386) 555-1439

I leaned back in my wooden desk chair; springs squealed as they grew taught. There was no mention of payment and nothing about our meeting. I checked my bank account there was an extra $300. I was assigned a case. They didn't teach me anything about this in PI school. Since I was broke, I went with it.

Places to start traveled across my brain. There were places to go and places to call to find this girl. After merely seconds of thought I hit a dead end. Suddenly the urge to steal a car and chop it for quick cash began to take over my thoughts. I walked through the steps of what to steal and where to chop it. Before I could spend the imaginary money, I switched gears again and reread the email and began to feel the desperation in the father's letter to a stranger to find his only child. If Gregg was not going to the cops for help, there was more to his story. Suddenly stealing cars was not so interesting.

The cell phone dinged once again.

"Hey Billy, I'm legit now. Got an office and everything." I said leaning back in a wooden desk chair I bought at an auction for five bucks.

"Aren't we all legit these days?" Billy chuckled as did I. Neither one could take the chance a phone was tapped. The statute of limitations had not run out on all the crimes we had committed. Then Billy added, "All I got to do is say when and you're there." Billy cracked a smile that sounded through the phone. I reciprocated knowing it was true.

"So, what's up?"

"What's up? You totally blew off our meeting with Smitty."

"I was busy, besides I told you I wasn't meeting with him. Didn't you hear me, I'm legit."

Billy sighed. Our friendship was going through some growing pains. We had only known each other as criminals, and we were no longer that. The teacher was losing a pupil.

"Well, there's some guy here at the shop looking for you. Says his name is Pope."

"Shit."

"You want me to get rid of him?"

"Nah, he's an Army buddy. Give him my address. I'll be here."

Billy's end of the call went scratchy then he said, "I'm not sure he can make it. You better come here." That was it, Billy hung up. I sat up and checked the phone. The call was done so I left.

Billy's current shop was not far, just up US 1, not giving me much time to contemplate what Pope was doing in town and why it was he couldn't make it the couple of miles to my office. The last I saw of Pope was that night I chose to run off into the darkness and Pope chose a military career.

The sun beat down and it was already in the 80's. I whipped the C-10 in and parked in the shade of the building. Pope was leaning against the north wall drinking from a black hose. The water barely getting into his mouth, cascading down his bearded chin and soaking into his tattered t-shirt and stained faded blue jeans. A pair of worn black tennis shoes were on the curb beside him.

Billy came out of the shadow of one of the bays with a red rag in his hands. He wiped them off then shook my hand. We both stood looking at Pope who seemed oblivious to the two of us watching him.

"He wandered up here asking to use my hose. I brought him inside for a coke, but he refused, just wanted the hose."

"Yeah, how'd I come up?"

"Oh, he saw a picture of you up on the office wall. You're in that sixty-nine Judge." Billy turned toward me, "Come see me before you leave."

I watched him walk back into the blackness of the shop bay.

"Hey Pope." I said as I approached my battle buddy, though I never finished A school Pope went on to have a career. And a career he had; Pope proved to be the bravest man I knew. He was a soldier who signed up to fight for God and country, unlike me. I needed an escape and putting time and distance between me and this town.

Last year I heard from Pope when he called telling me he had been medically discharged from the Army and did not know what to do with his life. He hoped I could help him out. I had just got back from my last job from Smitty, sitting on cash, just surfing the summer away. I had no solutions for a moral compass like Pope.

"Hey man." Pope put the hose down without turning it off. When he spoke, I noticed a black rotting front tooth. His neck and arms were a deep reddish-brown contrasting starkly with the white flesh beneath his shirt.

I stood silent. Closer now, I could see Pope was wearing a stained t-shirt with a faded logo. His jeans were too big for him and were held up with a belt synched tight. I took several seconds to blink. He looked around as if he had just got there even though he had been there for fifteen minutes or more. Then he said, "You got ta' help me."

I still said nothing. Pope's hands were grimy and his eyes bloodshot. The more immediate problem were needle marks in Pope's arms. He claimed to be clean, but the marks were only days old. The man was not the combat vet I remembered all those years ago. Pope was nearly 5'9" and currently about 115 pounds. His eyes were shallow with dark blue rings around them.

"Can we, like, go for a beer? I'm just so thirsty and I think…" Pope never finished his sentence. The cars passed up and down US 1 as we stood in the shade of the building. Billy moved a car in and out of the garage bay. A seagull landed and picked at something mushed on the light grey concrete.

I finally broke my silence, "Pope, you need to get help. Have you been to the VA?"

Pope scoffed, "The VA? Seriously Roger." His eyes would not stay put, they moved with every passing car. "Man can we just go for a beer, like old times?"

I pointed to my truck.

I left Pope in the truck with the A/C blasting while I went inside the office. Billy was there eating a sub sandwich. He put it down leaving black greasy smudges on the white bread. Still chewing, he said, "How's the truck?"

I nodded, "Good. The A/C probably needs a charge."

Billy wiped his mouth then said, "Well I can do it now. We still gotta get under that thing and finish the suspension. That rear end is probably all over the road."

"Now that I got a job, I'll have the money for the parts." I turned and started for the door.

"We got a lot of hours into that thing. Be a shame to not finish it." He took a big bite of his sub.

I paused as the door began to open itself. Standing there with neatly combed white hair was Smitty. He smiled, and the gold tooth gleamed even in the dim light of the office. His seventy-year-old eyes were bright as he extended a gold braceleted wrist and open hand.

I shook it softly as he clenched down. My bones began to touch in an unnatural way. Then he eased up.

"Take a seat." His raspy voice commanded. I felt like a kid in the principal's office.

Billy kept eating but refused to look me in the eye. The laces around my chest tightened and I struggled to control my breathing, keeping a cool demeanor was a must.

Smitty remained standing as I sat. "Roge," he was the only person to ever call me Roge and I hated it, "What's with dodging my calls?"

"I'm making a change for myself."

Smitty glanced over at Billy and nodded understandingly.

I continued, "That change is getting out of the business, trying something new on my own."

"Yeah, I know, Private Investigator, sure. I knew one back in the 80's, Mike or Mick, whatever. He was a good guy, looked in on some things for me and such. But you don't want to end up like that guy. Let me run something by you."

"I said I was out. I told you after I got pinched, I wasn't ever going to take that risk again." My voice remained calm though my brain was on fire.

"Sure, nine months, was it? I did seven years in Florida State Prison, only back then we called it East Unit. So don't cry me some bullshit about your lousy nine months in county."

"I don't like being trapped." I said, conviction trailing behind the words.

"Try living in an eight by ten cell with a guy who wants nothing more than to run a shive from your nuts to your chin and the only reason he don't is 'cause you got pals on the outside making sure of it. Guardian fucking angels."

Stale blue eyes locked onto mine. We clenched in a struggle. Finally, Smitty smiled, showing his gold tooth, and looked over at Billy. "Billy, it was good to see you." He turned back to me and shook his head, "Good luck kid."

"What ever happened to Mike?" I asked knowing I shouldn't.

"He got himself stabbed to death over on Main Street." Smitty said and walked out.

Billy had a mouth full of sub sandwich when he flipped the bird to the door as it closed behind Smitty. I stood to leave then spotted the picture Billy had mentioned of me stapled to the 'wall of fame' with twenty other pictures of hot cars that have come through the shop, legally. I ripped it off the wall.

"That's a liability," I said. We exchanged smiles and I walked out knowing things would be smooth with Billy again.

The first stop was back to the office. I had to get Pope into a clean shirt and shorts, before that, he had to wash up in the sink at the end of the hall. Pope stepped out grinning with the limited teeth he had left. He was swimming in the size large t-shirt and had to hold the shorts up with one hand. There was a time the large shirt would have been tight around the shoulders and arms. That hard-cut military body had been erased and redrawn into a stick figure.

"You look like shit but at least you don't smell like it." I pulled a belt from the cabinet drawer I got the other clothes.

His grin faded, "True. I thought we were close in size. You must a got fatter." Pope grinned again and so did I.

Pope passed for an average guy as we walked together down a block to Cooper's, an Irish themed pub. We passed through the large wooden door with worn brass handles, the inside was dim despite the light from fake kerosene lamps, due to the deep stain on all the wood trim. The bar ran the length of the south wall. It was stocked with a lot of whiskeys and a few other liquors. There were several beers on tap and a double door cooler filled with bottled craft brews. I had begun to enjoy Cooper's since maturing my taste buds and this became the place for that.

The mid-day lunch rush was over. A couple of guys wearing ties talked in loud whispers about office politics, what they would do if they were in charge and why Nancy was such a dumbass. I lead Pope towards the back. I decided it was best not to belly up to bar considering the topic of the conversation we were about to have.

Behind the bar was a long blond ponytail attached to a toned body wearing a tight green t-shirt and black shorts. I took a double take, but right then my body was working independently of my mind. I could feel myself coming out of hibernation and I wanted to eat. She turned with a familiar look, I knew her, and she knew me, but no idea from where.

Her smile was bright and her green eyes light up, stimulated on by the green shirt no doubt. We locked eyes for so long, I nearly walked into a bar stool.

She smiled as she said, "Take a seat wherever you like."

I pointed to an empty two top just off the end of the bar. We sat in silence. Pope looked around and nodded with approval. I supposed it was his choice of establishment as well.

"It's good to see you again man." I needed to fill the silence, a feeling I was not accustomed to but felt had to be done.

Pope shrugged, "Yeah man." His eyes darted like he was watching a Ping-Pong game.

I searched for the right words. As my mind was in pursuit of more words, my eyes acted independently and found what they wanted, the cute bartender as she came over.

"Hi, I'm Alysa, what are you drinking?" She said as she dropped off two menus. Pope had water and a domestic light beer. I ordered an oatmeal stout. As Alysa walked off, I could not help myself watch her go. A feeling that was distracting me from my friend's suffering had to be suppressed. *After*, I thought as I forced my eyes to Pope.

Pope sat still with a half-smile. He looked at the menu but did not open it. Up to the left of him a TV was on. He watched sports highlights being recapped as his mind searched for something to say. Once the water came, Pope gulped it down, dribbling as he swallowed. With the glass nearly empty he came up for air and to wipe his mouth. I did not want to look towards the bar.

"Easy man.", was all I said. My menu was open, but I was not planning to eat if Pope didn't.

"Yeah, I needed that. Whoa it's cold though." Pope grit his teeth as the ice-cold water momentarily froze the back of his brain. Pope had finally stopped sweating. I figured I would not be getting those clothes back. I was glad to give them. A bond existed between the two of us. We had survived a crucible together, the mental and physical hardships of basic training. Though I chose my own path that took me out of the Army, Pope stood by me, even writing the tribunal a letter endorsing the few good things I did as a solider. A debt existed that neither of us would acknowledge or would be filled or ever could be filled.

Alysa came back with the beers. She asked if we would be eating. I nodded. Pope remained silent and still. He did not have a cent in his borrowed pockets.

When Pope refused to speak, I said, "A couple of cheeseburgers and fries and we'll start with some onion rings." I felt a smile break my mouth apart as it worked muscles in my cheeks I rarely used.

Alysa smiled and said sure thing then paused before walking off, "Where do I know you from?"

My eyes peered over the pint glass as I sipped up the black stout. I swallowed, then I said, "Not sure. It's a small town." Alysa agreed and walked off. My statement had been half-truth and half lie. Daytona Beach was a small town compared to its neighbors, north and west, so that was true. The lie was that we had met, several times. Alysa had been a bartender for several years now, bouncing around the different hot spots that open and closed in a year. Being a small town with a healthy drinking problem, I showed up with the rest of town and eventually Alysa would serve me a drink. Our interactions never exceeded that of barkeep and patron.

Pope sipped his beer. He held his other hand out and watched the fingers quiver. Sweat broke out over his body. The shaking hand was laid flat on the table. "Thank you, I..."

"We'll get through this battle too, brother."

"Hey, I know," came Alysa's voice just over my shoulder forcing me to turn.

"Yeah?"

"You used to come see me at Sun Setters."

"Probably." I knew that to be true. This wasn't a game of hard to get, I just am hard to get because I don't care. Though Alysa was beautiful, friendly, and always treated me well when I visited her bar, I was not the relationship type. First, I was broke; it's hard to be romantic when you're broke. Second, I just swore off broads. The start of a new career required late nights, random hours and there was hopefully danger to come. And right now, she was just interrupting.

I turned back around to Pope who was picking up on my nerves beginning to fray with this hot bartender. A slight smile creased his eyes. A small tell only a man who has seen you fight for your life would know.

"Shut up." I whispered. Pope now knew I had not changed. I was same back then, always about the job. Not out of duty or fear of punishment (It was rumored I had no fear) but just something in me that I needed to be on task. So back on task it was.

"Tell me something man, who are you buying from?" I was looking at the TV when I asked.

Pope shifted in his seat. He gulped his beer down then let out a slight burp followed with a half grin to ease my tension, "What are you gonna do Grimes, kill all the dealers in town?"

His smile faded when he looked into my eyes.

I leaned in and said, "I'm no snake charmer, Pope. I find a snake I cut the head off."

Pope eyes rolled around the bar looking everywhere except across the table. "Here and there." He said under his breath.

"Nope. Try again."

"What are you gonna beat it outta me if I don't?" Pope held a smile that faded fast. It was the man in his eyes, that's how Pope knew not to mess with me.

I waited in silence, keeping my eyes on him though he wouldn't return the stare.

"Okay man," Pope said, then came the bartender again.

"Here you are boys. Piping hot so watch it." Her smile was infectious, but I had been inoculated.

"Yeah thanks," I said cold. I didn't look at her, I didn't want to. I knew what my eyes would say, and she didn't deserve that.

When she was gone, I said, "I want a name?"

"Lenny." Pope touched an onion ring and snapped his hand back like a viper was after it. "Shit's hot."

"Where do you find him?"

"I don't know man, around. Like I see him around and if I have cash I score."

"How much do you need?"

Pope crinkled his brow then scoffed a little letting out air. "What? Man, I'm getting clean, and you want to buy me stuff?" He shook his head trying to understand what I was after. It wasn't his fault; his brain must look like a yanked out wiring harness from an '85 Caddy. Just a mess.

I shook my head side to side. I grabbed an onion ring and blew on it then took a bite. It was hot but tolerable. The temperature was still too hot to get a good taste, but I knew from experience they were good. Having an office one block away from a pub was a double-edged sword now. Eat and drink great, get fat and spend money. I would have to balance on that blade.

When I did not say anything, Pope thought about what I was asking. His sober mind was working slower these days, but still working. The connections were being made. "Fuck don't Grimes."

I put the empty pint down. My head was slightly cocked to the left, my eyes still and focused. "It's the only way."

Pope looked down at his shaking hands, hands that used to hold an M4 so still he could drop a man at 500 yards. A chest pinned with medals was replaced with an arm pinned with needles. The man who could bring him back was sitting across the table and all I needed was a location.

"3rd street." He said looking me in the eyes with a reserve that up until now had been depleted.

Alysa showed up again right on queue to interrupt. "Two burgers." She was indeed a good barkeep and knew the two of us were discussing something deeper than why Nancy was such a fuck up. This conversation had consequences and Alysa knew she needed to give us space and more beer. She left with the empty pints and refilled them without asking.

My eyes drifted down to the worn exposed pine floor of the pub. A couple of pints in and my mind was putting the pieces together more fluidly, filling in gaps with assumptions. Pope did not know how exact the information he was giving up was by letting me know it was on 3rd street that he bought his smack. There was only one real gang in town, and they ran 3rd street, in fact that was their name. I knew them by name, by reputation and by having gone to high school with a few of them.

There was a time when I was just learning the craft of stealing cars under the ever-careful tutelage of Billy when one of the guys from 3rd approached me about stealing a car for him. It was his mom's car, she was underwater in it and that is just where the dude wanted the car, under water. The young gangbanger's name was D'Marcus Jones. He wasn't particularly big or scary, at least not when standing alone. It was when he had two or three of his gangbangers with him that I began to feel the pressure.

I was not sure how D'Marcus had found out about me stealing cars. Maybe it was just one criminal recognizing another but somehow, he knew. See, Billy's number one rule was not to shit where you eat. We never stole a car in our own county. This was all still new for the young junior in high school, and I had never boosted a car without Billy near. I knew Billy would flip his shit but the alternative to angry Billy was getting the beating of a lifetime. Sure, even in high school I was tough, but it would not end with one beat down and I knew that. I fight today, I fight every day. So, Mrs. Jones's Lincoln Town car sank into the Halifax River.

D'Marcus and I avoided each other for a little while. Later, D'Marcus tried to get more out of me. In my naiveté I thought there was some honor or code between us, and he owed me one. D'Marcus was too dumb to realize he needed me as an ally, instead he tried to use fear to intimidate me, which was not going to work. That is when I learned I was not a man to be leaned on.

It only took a week before D'Marcus and two of his associates cornered me to pull another job, I refused. So, they made threats. I decided to force the threat. I pushed past D'Marcus and threw a flying punch at the bigger of the two men standing behind D'Marcus. The man crumpled. I then straight leg kicked the other sending him over. D'Marcus did all the talking after that, he said we were good. That was it, he avoided me the rest of high school. D'Marcus went on to establish himself with 3rd St. I went on to steal cars and more. I learned there was no loyalty or street code between us. D'Marcus didn't see himself as owing me a favor. That was too bad, I could use a favor on this before it turned around and bit me in the ass.

A little tickle started, more of a tingle, which moved out of my chest down each arm. My breathing increased just enough to take notice. I felt my eyes widen, and then I knew what was coming. There, sitting across from me was hard work. Now I had looked ahead three steps, I had to see the finished product, Pope would get clean and get his life back.

"Hey man." Pope sat with a confused grin.

I was staring out into nothing, lost in the planning of my new mission in life, getting Pope clean. It paid nothing and could get me killed; I was alright with that. Pope wondered if his savior here was just as messed up as he was. I did too. Going after drug dealers was stupid. It wasn't the kind of thing to do in the spur of the moment. Planning, surveillance, and most of all guns were needed.

"You alright?"

I shook the idea out of my head. Alysa appeared with two beers, "Now I know you. From Ocean Side, right?"

Her beauty held my slippery tongue and I smiled, "I thought it was Sun Setters, but yeah, I've been to Ocean Side. I don't like it there."

The bartender's smile faded as she put the beers down. Pope smirked again as he regained feeling in his chest and remembered how much he had enjoyed my dryness. After basic and our first furlough, I had proved myself to be the unit's worst wingman. Every guy in the battalion hated to have a beer with me if the goal was picking up chicks and it always was. Natural good looks and my blue eyes always brought the girls around, but that viper tongue and lack of interest would scare them off.

"Dude, you haven't changed." Pope laughed and clinked his pint glass against mine. "And don't, buddy cause you're one in a million."

Chapter 3

That's the problem with living in a toilet bowl. You're always swirling around with the same old shit. If I'm going down the drain, I might as well take the shit with me.

Pope lay on the couch in the dark office. His head was turned to his right with his chin touching his shoulder. A light whistle came from his nose as he breathed in an out. Much needed repairs were taking place on the cellular level while he slept. His hands twitched periodically, the last remanence of the toxins leaving his system. Moments ago, I was holding his weak head above the porcelain rim as he heaved and heaved with no results. It had been a messy two days, the sweating, vomiting and anxiety. When he wakes his cravings will only be worse.

I sat at my desk with heavy eyes. Very little sleep in two days. I hadn't checked my messages or emails in that time. Sanford was checking in on the case he sent over. I lunged forward in the chair. The business was open and burning through what little cash I held onto. The lawyer with the retainer could cut me off at any moment. This was it; this was all I had and I was screwing it up. Money had to come in from somewhere or else the lights went out on Grimes Investigations. And that meant something I swore I would never do again. It was a tough walk keeping on the right side of the law.

Years ago, after leaving Pope and the army, I was back in my hometown around the people that had taught me to get away with it, that little scratching, wanton gnawing at my insides started. The only way to get it to stop was to steal something. The problem with that-is, like Pope and his need for heroin; it had to be more, more than the last score. I had to break those old habits and build new, build on something that would force me to give that up and go legit. Still, like one of Pope's dirty needles, the sting of being broke remained.

After reading Gregg Hines's email wanting me to find his daughter, I was standing in front of the window, staring out at a moonless night. The city lights split in two by a dark swath that was the inner coastal river. Across the river on the beach side the lights were brighter and higher than on this side. The biggest glow came from the boardwalk and pier, giving light to tourists and locals alike. There were pickpockets wandering up and down the boardwalk picking a mark. Mixed in among them were drug dealers, mingling with tourists looking to get high. And curled in the shadows of the towering hotels were runaways from all over.

"Hey brother," Pope's weak voice scraped over an acid burned throat came to me in the dark.

I didn't turn but held my focus on the city lights knowing below were the hookers and the pushers, the death dealers making a quiet city sick.

"Remember that time I came to see you while on leave?"

"Which time?" I replied.

"The first time. Man, that was fun. I had just made Corporal was about to deploy. Remember that? We hit the clubs and bars and I got so hung over, I was so sick. Man, you took care of me then, got me an IV from that cute nurse you knew. Hey what ever happened to that girl?"

"She went to prison and I kinda lost touch with her." I took a seat at my desk and poured some bourbon into a glass. It burned as it went down.

"What for?" Pope asked as he struggled to lift his head. He gave up and just laid back.

"She was patching up gunshot wounds from some guys in a local MC, they had a beef with some other club and got shot up. Cops busted her for not reporting it."

"That was the best week of my life buddy, the best. Thanks for that man. I thought about that week when I was deployed, a lot brother, like all the time." Pope shut his eyes and his breath slipped into a smooth rhythm.

I turned and looked at Pope one more time. His skeletal body lay sprawled on the couch. During basic training he had lost a significant amount of weight. He was a cheese puff eating gamer who thought this was going to be the most real game of Call of Duty in his life. I had already started MMA training but was still far from where I needed to be in those days. Pope was strong, not just in his muscles but in his gut. That inner strength pushed him when his legs gave out on seven mile runs or crawling through mud while being shouted between grenade explosions. It wasn't something I had.

Steeling had been in my blood, just as heroin was running in Pope's. Cars, smash and grabs, home break ins, those kinds of things. They were quick, get in get out, kind of pace that made twelve weeks of bootcamp endless. And the accompanying four-year enlistment just not possible. I did what I knew how to do and stole a Humvee. The only thing that saved me from prison time and a dishonorable was the Colonel who parked it, parked it in front of his subordinate's quarters after hours. She wanted the whole thing, including me to go away.

Pope survived and went on to survive multiple tours. Now cheap smack was his undoing. He tried to help me break my own cycle, to cut the selfishness out of me and be a force to help others. Twelve years later I found it somewhere in my gut to make a change. Now I needed to repay him.

In a hidden compartment, under the desk, was a drawer with tools, tools used in robberies. Glass cutter, wire cutters, gloves, screw drivers and a code scanner for keypads. The metal file cabinet across from the desk held other tools. In the bottom drawer was a long rectangular case. Inside the case were foam cutouts that held a few pistols, magazines, suppressors, and a collapsible baton. On the floor of the closet was a large duffel bag that held my entire wardrobe. Various folded shirts and pants, all black. There was one last thing weighing down the bottom of that bag, a Kevlar vest.

Everything I needed to wage a war on the drug pushers in the city. That isn't what I do. My job is to find a missing girl and her father is relying on me to do it.

An afternoon storm had finished its roll through town and took some humidity with it. Even with the breeze coming off the ocean left it too warm. The humidity glued the salt to my skin as I wandered up and down the concrete walk along the ocean.

It was just after eight and the crowd of tourists and locals reached its peak which wasn't much. Some people walked along the wet sands of the outgoing tide while others licked dripping ice cream cones outside the arcade. I took a seat on a thick slab of concrete that made up a section of sea wall and began to people watch.

Not long into the show a few bottom feeding urchins emerged to find easy tourist marks along the boardwalk. One guy, skinny and dirty around the edges, passed the same couple a few times, circling around and coming back. The man and woman stood in line for a beer at the window of an arcade. The girl behind the counter made eye contact with the urchin a couple times then nodded just before spilling a freshly poured beer. The urchin made his move.

The vacationing man leapt back bumping into the skinny man. The skinny urchin accepted the man's apology with a smile and a quick pat down. I watched the wallet transfer pockets. Then the skinny urchin was off. The girl behind the counter poured another beer and waved off any form of payment. The couple went on with their vacation.

The same scene played out but in different ways for the next few hours. At around ten, one of the restaurants on the beach began to thump some bass as multi-colored lights flashed in the window signaling a two for one special and locals get in free until eleven. I sat still. It was a good seat to watch the entire boardwalk.

Groups of teens walked back and forth, laughing, and talking fast. Most painted in a juicy rare, broiled by the days sun. I couldn't find a match of long brown hair, braces, or light splatter of freckles in any of the faces that passed by.

After a second lap around the arcade, I was starting to catch the eye of heavy blond with beading moisture around her mouth. She was standing behind the prize counter filled with cheap toys worth a fraction of what it took to win them. It was time to talk to the employees before one of them called the cops.

"It's a long shot, but have you seen this girl?" I held the phone for her.

With a finger and thumb, she wiped the sweat from the corners of her mouth then squinted at the phone.

"Hard to say. We get so many you know." She folded her arms over a bulging midsection and leaned on the glass counter.

"So many what?"

She straightened up, "You aint with the police?"

I'd never been mistaken for a police officer before, "No. I'm a private investigator." I started to pull my wallet, but she waved it off.

"Oh, I guess it were two nights ago some plain clothes cops came looking for a missing girl too."

"This girl?" I held the phone up. She didn't look.

"Nah, this one were blond and maybe a year or two older. Out of towner, I think. You're girl an outta towner?"

"No, local." I looked out at the sea of blinking lights as the chatter of winners and losers carried over me. "Can I leave my number in case you spot her?"

She tore off some receipt paper and handed it over along with a pen. She pulled a stack of business cards paperclipped together. The one on top had a badge embossed on it and clipped the receipt over it.

"We get them in from time to time." She said then went back to wiping down the smudges and smears left by excited kids claiming their prizes.

I returned to the slab of concrete. I was in the right spot but maybe on the wrong night. There had to be a better way of tracking Milo down, if she was even still in Daytona or Florida for that matter. Hines didn't want me to go to the cops. He wanted his name kept out of the papers. The ultimate in selfishness. His own daughter missing and he's more worried about his image.

By about eleven thirty the crowd thinned of teenagers and an older sort began filling the gaps. The lights to the rides went off and a few of the shops began pulling their mannequins in and shutting their doors. The restaurant across from me changed too. The lights dimmed as colored lights began to spin with the elevated bass from somewhere inside.

A young guy dressed in saggy jean shorts and high-tops stood just off to the side of the door to the restaurant. Most of the time he kept his head down, twisting the young dreadlocks sprouting from his scalp. The man paced around and made eye contact every so often with people going in and out of the club. More than once he was approached and after a few *yeps* and head bobs the potential client walked away without an exchange. Either the kid was new or not good at his job. When an exchange did happen, it was the standard handshake and then the person would leave with something from the man's back pocket. I managed a couple of cellphone pics that when zoomed in, just got fuzzier.

I took the large concrete steps up to the main road and found there was still ten minutes left in the meter. I sat and watched the people of all kinds move along. None of them resembled Milo. The key was in the ignition ready to turn when the young drug dealer popped up from the stairwells. I watched him walk to the intersection and cross A1A. Halfway out of the truck I remembered I didn't bring my mask. As he got further from me the urge to follow was winning then I remembered I had a camo-colored Gaiter in my glove box and slipped it in my pocket.

After a couple more blocks, I closed the gap. It would take more than a few fuzzy cell phone pictures to prove he was dealing. At a stretch of darkness between streetlamps, I rolled the Gaiter over my face and charged. The man never heard me coming but felt the blow as two arms wrapped around his mid-section and pushed him forward off his feet. It happened so fast and hard the young man came out of his poorly laced Jordan's.

The impact on the coquina asphalt skinned both the man's knees and one elbow. His cell phone bounced off the asphalt and slid to the gutter. By the time the young drug dealer knew what was happening, I already had him in a submission hold. Barely breathing the man said, "Yo, what the fuck? Let me up."

"No fighting, understand?" I tightened my grip forcing air from the man's lungs. The guy nodded he understood and would comply. I let him up slowly.

I pushed the man off the sidewalk and got him moved to the dark side of a single-story house with a for sale sign posted in the yard. There in the shadow of the house a series of cuss words dribbled from the drug dealer's mouth as he inspected his knees and elbow. Then he saw his phone. "Aw c'mon man."

"Empty your pockets."

I could tell the guy was young and hadn't been doing this long by the way he complied. There was little point in resisting or fleeing, he was already beaten by the man commanding him. Hell, he didn't even want to be a drug dealer anyway.

"Yo, you mugging me?"

"Yes." I grabbed a wad of cash from the dealer's open palm.

"This isn't even my money; I'm just filling in." The young man went on with a string of cuss words. Then he said something about what would happen to him when he showed up with no drugs and no money.

I let him ramble on as I counted out the money, $225 and one small plastic wrapped packet of coke. I tossed the coke and pocketed the cash.

"I want to know who sells heroin on the boardwalk?" My voice came out strained.

"Aw c'mon man. I don't do this. Like only once before. I'm just helping my dog out."

I grabbed the man at the elbow, digging my thumb into the soft inside of the joint. A groan filled the darkness. The man went weak in the knees and almost went down. I let up a little and the man stood.

"Yo, please man. Just take the cash and go." His eyes were squinted and glassy. If it wasn't for the smell of fear, I would think he had been laughing all this time.

I squeezed on his joint once more. He squealed.

"His name." I grunted in his face so he could feel my hot breath.

"T-bag." He sniffled.

"What?"

"I know. He's a dumb ass." He said with the fight in him gone. He began to calm now that he spilled his guts.

"Where is he now?"

"Aw fuck. C'mon don't do me like this." The sniffling began again.

"Give him up and you walk on your own. If you don't, I'll break your elbow. You know when you break your elbow, they can't set it right? You just got to let it heal and not break it again."

"Evergreen Place off Dixon. Apartment three." When he finished, I let him go. He nearly dropped but caught himself by holding onto the wall.

We stood in the shadows between the houses. Light from the street caught the roof tops but left us covered in night, sunken in the small concrete canyon. I could hear the rap-a-tap of a sprinkler going back and forth. The street was empty. The kid wiped his nose. I needed more from him.

"And who gives T-bag his orders?"

The kid looked at me like I had two heads with its for eyes. "What? You wanna die? Ppssff, white people." He said shaking his head.

This time all I had to do was shift my weight and the kid caught on to what was coming. He spat out, "Delroy."

"Delroy what?"

"Antus, I think. Don't ask me to spell it." The man wouldn't look me in the eyes after he gave up the boss.

I took my eyes off James for a second to scan the street. It was still and dark. Not a single car had passed since I began my assault on the drug dealer.

"Your name?"

"James." His eyes went glassy again, "Now what, my address so you can come to my house if you ever see me out here again?"

"You watch a lot of superhero movies don't you Jimmy?"

"Ppssff, shit." James looked around at the empty street. There was no help coming. "I guess."

"I don't want your address. I want to know where I can find Delroy."

"You crazy man. Delroy isn't someone you want to mess with okay." He paused, waiting for me to come back with something witty. James did watch a lot of action movies especially superhero ones. As the man in the mask, I said nothing, just watched and took in every move James made.

"I really don't know."

"What does he drive?"

"I don't know man, I ain't his chauffeur." His eyes slowly met up with mine. My mouth did not move, but my eyes told him to keep talking. "Okay, a black Infiniti on gold dubs man."

Satisfied with the interrogation, I tossed the coke on the roof of the house and put the cash in my pocket, a nice little saving account for Pope. James barely protested, only mumbling about the beating he will be getting thanks to this dick in a mask. I didn't care, despite thinking Jimmy was an alright kid. I could tell by the way he talked and walked he was no gang banger. The kid, if applied, might do more in his life. None of that hope mattered now. All that mattered was him not tipping Delroy off before I could get to him.

In the same graveled voice, I said, "Turn around."

James started to sniffle; the realization that playing a drug dealer for real was a mistake. He went back in his mind at all the missed opportunities to tell T-bag no, but that was like telling Delroy no and no one tells Delroy no. In that moment, anticipating the bang of a pistol and the subsequent bullet through his brain, he hated Delroy more than the man about to kill him. "I hate Delroy, you better make him suffer for this." James went down on his knees.

I was standing, holding zip ties in my hand, not a pistol. "Get up. I'm not going to kill you."

James waited a moment then turned slowly. With no pistol brandished, he got to his feet, there was a small grin beginning to stretch across his dark face.

"But this is gonna hurt." I threw a right. James felt his knees give as he hit the wall and slid to the lush St. Augustine grass. The dew on the grass cooled the burn of my fist on his face. He wasn't out but he wasn't getting up either. His arms were limp as I bound his wrists with the ties, then his ankles.

I stood over him, "If you really want Delroy to pay then don't go back to his hood. Don't talk to any of his friends and whatever you do, don't stand too close to him because I'm coming for him." I turned my back to James, as I walked into the light in the street, I pulled the mask off and jogged away, stopping to pick up the kid's cellphone.

James sat in the shadow of the house with a smile, there was that superhero talk he was waiting for.

I sat in my truck with it running. My limbs were on fire, and I was breathing heavy, not from the jog back but from what would be, what I was getting myself into. The sheer anticipation was bubbling up filling my veins and speeding up my heart. Oh, this was going to be fun. The last six months had been nothing but a bore, a time filler leading up to now. I was wasting my life surfing and spending the cash I made all just distractions to keep from stealing again. The straight and narrow was nothing but a tomb, a place to rest tired bones, not bones on fire. That tingle needed a scratch. Like a junkie thief, the only to fix it would be to steal all the money and drugs I could.

Pope, I had forgotten about Pope. He was back at my office sound asleep. He would wake up with cravings he could not curb. Today was alright, but tomorrow would turn to hell for the addict. The cravings in me were just as strong. The only way to curb them would be to collect evidence on the drug operation and turn it over to the cops. I had to cut the head off the snake that was feeding him that venom. And I had to do it tonight.

Stopping back at the office, Pope was still asleep. I grabbed my duffle bag and headed out for the Evergreen apartments It was a plain looking two story apartment complex. Beige on the sides with a dark green tile roof meant to compliment the golf course just beyond the apartments. I'm sure back in the 1960's when the course was still private and segregated these apartments were stylish and attracted swinging bachelors. Today it was mostly Section 8 single mothers of five.

I circled around the parking lot getting an idea of the lay out. The odd numbered apartments were upstairs, I didn't like that. I was left without options, and I wanted at T-bag tonight. There was something about a guy who was dumb enough to call himself T-bag that just made me ball a fist and punch in the face. I knew it would feel good. It would also feel good knowing this shit bag was about to get taken off the streets. People like Pope and others would hopefully be sober enough after tonight to make a change in their lives. I had made a change too, from career criminal to upright private eye. All addicts are expected to relapse, and I was about to.

A light came on framing the window of apartment three in white. At the same time headlights blinded me. I pinched my eyes and sunk low in the seat as an Infiniti on twenty-two-inch rims rolled slowing over the speed bump, bass thumping softly from the trunk. The windows tinted black so the car may have been driving itself.

The door to apartment three opened. A tall skinny dude in a t-shirt and long jean shorts shuffled out. He took the stairs down and went up to the Infiniti. I had my camera out with the red record button on.

Hands were exchanged, so was light conversation. Then the car left. I let the camera record T-bag all the way until he was inside again. Quickly I played it back. Dark and grainy. Pausing and zooming in on the exchange helped but was it enough?

T-bag had the proof, I just needed to get it. I went up the stairs, crouching low, crab walking just beneath the windows until I got to his. From the corner of the blinds, I focused the lens of my camera and recorded. From the tiny screen I could see the corner of a coffee table and a couch with T-bag's legs coming off it. His hands were counting cash, laying bills one on the other. A small baggy full of what had to be weed and two small bags of white powder, just like the one I took off James accompanied it.

A car door slammed somewhere below. Lying flat on the concrete walk, my ears perked. Shoes scraped against the concrete steps coming my way.

Hands pulling along the walk, toes barely touching, I hurried to the opposite stairwell just as the new arrival appeared. With my back against the wall, controlling my breathing, I poked the camera out.

A small figure in a hoodie and tight shorts knocked on T-bags door. It opened and closed. Another deal? Another pay out from a small timer like James?

Back on all fours, I crawled to the window.

All I could see were two sets of legs now coming from the couch. Nothing much happened for several minutes until the smaller set of legs wrapped around the larger set.

This wasn't what I came for, so I turned the camera off and sat with my back against the wall, just under the window.

Instead of pulling out and heading to US 1, I went the other way, deeper into the neighborhood wondering what I might find. Winding crisscross streets lined with ranch style homes that all looked the same caught me in a suburban web. The houses were single story, garage on the left or right and white door in the front. Most of the lawns were dead except for the one house with the over decorated lawn of white nude statues and heavy white bars over every window. I figured the owner had the couch wrapped in plastic. The rest of the houses had cars on blocks and couches on porches.

After passing the same cop car for another time, I thought it was best to find my way out. A white guy circling this neighborhood in the middle of the night was a bullseye for any patrolman. I just didn't fit.

The patrol car swung around and sped up to get close on my tail. There was no doubt the license was about to be run. It would come back clear so there were no worries, but if those lights come on it will attract attention and lead to questions. My old life took over, as a plausible story to me being here filled my head. The PI license, that would get me out of this, but this is just what I wanted. I had evidence of a drug deal. This cop already knew who these dealers were and would be happy to take my evidence in, get a warrant and bust the dealers. After years of avoiding cops, this was the first time I was happy to see one.

I slowed and pulled over. I was quick to pull my wallet and toss it on the dash then kept my hands clearly on the wheel.

A minute later there was a flashlight beam in my face while the cop asked for identification. I felt the thickness of the Glock under my thigh. I took control, a calmness descended, allowing me to reach forward with a steady hand and pull the wallet open. I handed over the driver's license and the Private Investigator's license.

The officer was short. Her face held a permanent frown, jowls hanging like a bulldog face. Though her face was smooth, the uniform made her look older, mid-thirties I guessed. She had on a black ball cap with gold letters across it, *SHERIFF*. I recognized that bulldog face, it was Deputy Rhoshanda Camp, the one that sent me to jail. Shit. The cop tucked the light into her armpit and examined the license. She said nothing and walked back to her squad car.

I sat without moving my hands for several minutes. This was my first interaction with the police since becoming a legitimate private investigator. My eyes were wide, and my knee bounced as I waited for the cop to return. With my one prior conviction she would get me out of the car, and we would be here all night while she ripped out my newly installed interior.

The deputy came back and handed over the cards.

"I recognized your face." Camp said, handing me back my identification. She pushed the cap back on her forehead.

"Same here."

"That PI badge seems legit, checks out. How the hell did you manage one of those?"

"You got me on a misdemeanor. I can still be a PI in Florida." I forced a soft smile, nothing devilish or pride full.

"Well," She held her breath and then let it out, "I hope this means you've turned your shit around. I guess it takes a shit bag to catch a shit bag kinda thing in your line of work." Camp held nothing back on her feelings of Private Investigators. I can't blame her, I was playing cop, doing the gutter work they were too proud to get their badges tarnished doing.

"You working a case?" The bulldog faced cop mustered from pouty jowls. She bounced the light through the cab of my truck hoping to catch something she hadn't seen with the giant spotlight.

"Yep." I wanted out of there.

"What's the case about?"

"Drug dealers."

"Oh, drug dealers, really?" Sarcasm with a hint of condescension.

I started for the camera, and she started for the pistol grip. I stopped.

"I recorded a deal go down." I reached for the camera and paused. Slowly I looked back at her and her hand on that pistol.

She nodded and I grabbed the camera off the passenger seat. I held it while she squinted at the small screen and fuzzy images.

"Hmmm."

"I can give you the address and –"

"Let me stop you right there. This is, well, nothing. Your license lets you ask questions and spy on people, not enforce law. If you want to bust drug dealers, become a cop."

"I'm handing you a drug bust on a silver platter and you're just going to dismiss it? How about you do *your job*, Deputy. I did mine."

The cop cocked her head like a dog hearing the word 'treat'. She shifted her weight, and the free hand ran a thumb along her waste under the gun belt. Her body tensed; she was deciding how far she wanted to get into this with me.

"Okay, fine, since busting you did my career a solid, I'll do you a solid," She reached in her shirt pocket and pulled a business card. I took it, looked at her name and number then put it on the seat.

"You, ah, see any real crime or things get too hot for you, call me." Her voice was sincere. She walked back to her squad car.

I fired up my truck and pulled out.

Sitting in a 7-11 parking lot with the windows down, sucking on a Slurpee, Camps' condescending words played over and over. Each time harsher than the last. Her chuckling face and accompanying deputies as she recounted the story filled my head. None of them lifting a finger to stop the drugs and the damage it was causing.

It was up to me to do something, to make a dent in the Daytona drug trade. Being a PI wasn't enough, the cops didn't take me other any of this serious. I would get to the source, find out who is suppling one dealer, up the chain until I had them all. Getting in would be easy, I could shoot, and I could fight. Covering my tracks was my specialty.

Before the Slurpee was gone, I was back in the Evergreen parking lot staring up at the window of Apartment three. I pulled the long sleeve shirt over my vest. I wasn't taking chances on this one. Next, I screwed on the suppressor to the Glock 19. I closed the door to my truck as quietly as I could. The mask I wore was rolled up on top of my head and would easily be pulled down. I palmed my Glock, keeping it concealed to a casual observer, if there were to be one.

As I ascended the stairs I could hear a TV on full blast, just an infomercial selling a stain remover. T-bag's landlord will be needing some of that. At the top of the stairs, Apartment three was the second door to my left. Looking out over the railing at the parking lot, the only thing moving was a cat. He strolled through the still and quiet lot, sitting in the middle to lick his balls. Cats are such arrogant flea bags. I don't know whether to love him for the arrogance or kill him for it. I moved on.

With a palm pressed against the door I felt for sound. There was nothing. At this time of night there was a good chance he was not home. I would have better luck coming back about eleven in the morning but what I was about to do was better left done in the dark. Next, I felt the knob. It was loose but the dead bolt was through the jam.

My only option at this point is to put my lock picking skills into use. My mask was down over my face. I'm forced to stick the Glock under my left armpit and work the pick set into the lock. The mechanism was sloppy, it twisted and slid back easy, maintenance must change these out a lot. As soon as the lock went back, I right gripped the Glock and held my breath. No sound, no movement. I pushed the door open.

It was dark except for a dim yellow light coming from the kitchen to the left and behind the living room. To the right is a dark hallway. The carpet was plush as I entered and closed the door behind me. The smell of weed filled my nostrils but did not overpower my smell, the smell of the hunt that goes beyond my nose and through my pours, every nerve was on fire with anticipation for the kill. I fought the blood lust and beat it back into my heart. I needed coolness, a collected reserve to take over so I don't screw up.

The hallway was dark. As I passed the air handler it rattled. There was one door to my left and one to my right and both were closed. I didn't like the layout. It left me open, my back exposed. Light from under the door to my right showed on my feet. Time to play the odds.

I kicked the door to my right open. Inside there was just a dresser, lamp on the floor and next to it a mattress with two people in it, a man and woman. Both were naked and both responded slowly, slower than I wanted, making it tough to work with. I shouted, "Don't move."

They stayed still. I saw the man's hands go up. He's been here before. Without fully leaving the room I extended my long leg and kick the other door open. A dark bathroom. It was clear. I focused on the couple now gaining some sort of consciousness as they rose from drugged slumber. The girl was already face down in the pillow and I told her to stay that way. I closed the distance between us and whipped back the sheet. Both bodies were nude.

With the pistol pointed at T-bag, I growled, "Get up." He was slow but moved accordingly. His feet came over the side of the mattress and touched the stained tan carpet. My eyes flickered between him and the broad who so far, I couldn't tell was awake or not. T-bag was good, as my eyes looked back to him, I saw his hand had slipped under the pillow. Quickly I shoved the suppressor under his nose.

"Slow," I said. He listened and moved his hand out slower than molasses. Attached to it was a HiPoint 9 mm. His fingers were wrapped around the grip with none daring to cross the trigger guard. He dropped it on the carpet. I kicked it away. She still had not moved. I thought of Pope, and I wanted T-bag to bleed. So, I smacked him with the steel of the pistol, and he bled.

T-bag talked even though I hadn't asked any questions. "I got about a pound in the closet and two grand in the bottom drawer of the dresser. Just take it. I didn't know Delroy needed it…take it all." He babbled on but I didn't care. I was there to make him pay a debt to a war hero. A brother that had saved my life, now I needed to save his and this was all I could think of doing.

The suppressor pressed against the dark skin of T-bag's chest. He sniffled as his lip quivered. The girl lay still, either she had passed out or a total pro. I wasn't taking chances. My left hand shot and twisted; T-bag's eyes rolled as he fell back against his pillow. The girl stirred.

Her hair was a deep copper, wild and kinky, with the tip's blond. I heard a móan as she rolled over and I'm glad I had on a mask as her sleepy eyes judged mine. With a gasp, she said, "Oh." Her hands went out for the sheet, but it wasn't there.

In that instance, I noticed her age. The calm and collectedness told me she's a pro, been here before but I can't get past her face. That young roundedness of her eyes, and breasts that sat high on her chest, it made me want to look away out of modesty but I'm a pro too. The barrel remained fixed looking for a reason to go off.

She's just a kid. I heard in my mind as she watched my hands, especially my gun hand. The reasoning voice made me hate this bleeding shit-bag more. The girl couldn't be more than fifteen, and I'm sick for having seen her in this way, the way she was. I wanted to back out of there as a rewind and wash away what I just saw.

"Get up." I said through the mask, and she followed the command with ease. She turned her back to me in a jest at modesty. I played along and let her slip into her clothes which was just a pair of sweatpants and hoodie.

"Go." I grumbled and she scooted. I couldn't bring myself to hurt a young girl, even if she could identify me. Those soft brown eyes brought me back to that bank robbery and the day I left crime behind. I shook regret off and hoped sparing her life would somehow balance out some kind of cosmic scale in the universe and let me off for some of the things I have done. I won't think beyond *universe* because if I were to admit to a higher power then I know my sentence. I would be judged as I have judged others, and that sentence would be death.

The front door to the apartment closed behind her, I was left alone with T-bag. He was sitting up again in the bed; his head was in his hands. This wasn't an emergency for him, his breathing was steady, almost shallow.

"I'm not looking for weed. I want H, I want the heroin you've been selling on the streets."

I towered over him, unmoving. I convinced myself Pope needed me to do this, that he would be cured if I squeezed the trigger.

My finger wouldn't tighten, the trigger was still. T-bag's eyes went large, he held his breath. His mouth was open and moving, but no words escaped. I still could not pull that trigger. With a frustrating grunt my elbow twitched and back-handed the square edge of the Glock slide on T-bag's forehead, leaving a bloody furrow. He twisted as he fell into the bed. Both hands were over his forehead when he turned back, looking up at me as blood seeped from between his fingers.

My guts turned as thoughts clouded my actions, slowing my nerves. Reason pushed through the rage I had when I entered the apartment. Reason began telling me killing T-bag would not cure Pope. There are others, the dope snake has many heads and cutting of this little one won't kill it. My palm, wrapped tight around the pistol grip, began to sweat. I felt beads roll down my back and the mask absorbed all but from around my eyes as they burned with the salty sweat.

"Get up," I said. T-bag hesitated and then did what he was told. He stood and I realized he was taller than me but probably fifteen pounds lighter than I am. His hands came down slowly to his sides. He was breathing again; the oxygen was making its way to his brain, and he was thinking. I didn't like the look on his face, he was going to make a move, and the hunter in me regained control. I had to snap out of trying to save the planet and take this bastard down.

"Move." I pointed the pistol towards the door. He started to move past me, that's when I saw his muscle tense, the break was coming. He was fast but I was faster. My foot went out and connected with his knee, bending it forward as he went sideways. His other leg moved quickly to catch his fall but my forearm to his back hurried his descent and fell into the hallway. He tried once more to scramble but I was on his back. My right arm wrapped around his neck, my hand grabbing my left bicep. My left hand slipped behind his head. I tightened and he went limp.

I left T-bag in the corner of his bedroom as I began to ransack the place. First to the closet where I pulled out the weed. It is useless to me so that would get flushed. His dresser was next. It was made of cheap pressed wood with a pealing wood sticker laminate. I pulled out all five drawers. In the top drawer there were two stacks of rubber banded bills. They went into my pockets. I picked up the remaining drawers and flip the contents out on the bed. The next two held nothing but clothes. The last one was the same but felt heavier. Once flipped, I spotted why. Beneath it were tapped Ziploc bags of dope, all individually wrapped and ready for sale. My timing was perfect.

T-bag stirred in the corner. He was coming to, and I had some questions.

I slapped him lightly across the face, "Hey, wake up. I want to know who else around town deals for Delroy?"

His eyes rolled into focus. They were round and scared as his brain recharged, catching up on what just happened. He mumbled, but I didn't know what he said so I smacked him again and asked again.

"Um, ah, Delroy got a crew. There's Ja'Quawn and um. Shit you gonna kill me?" his eyes redden and began to fill with tears. T-bag's lip quivered, and I bet he looked like that when he was five. His fingers curled up into light fists that pounded down on is bare knees. I wondered what was with these guys. James cried and now T-Bag. Instead of pity it made me all the angrier.

I held my jaw tight as I said, "I'll make you a deal, T-bag. If you stop working for Delroy, I'll let you live. If I see you dealing again, you're dead."

T-bag nodded in compliance though I knew it to be a lie. I could see the lie in his eyes, at that moment he meant it to be true but when the fear subsided, he would fill the void with anger. He was not like James that anger would solidify his bond with Delroy, and they would be after me. I would have to stay ahead of them and strike fast. Without thinking it through, I just planned out the rest of my night.

"Now to show you I mean it." I grabbed one of his hands. He fought but lost at the tug-o-war. I pried back his index finger and snapped it like a celery stick, leaving it hanging. Saliva sprayed out as he screamed with a wide-open mouth.

I let his nerves do their job and shriek at him from inside his finger. Then I snatched the next one on his left hand. "Look at me T-bag, come on look."

T-bag refused to look at me. He buried his head in the corner.

"Who deals heroin?" I tightened my grip on his finger. His breathing increased as he turned his head further from me. "Who?" I said and began to bend the finger back.

An eerie whine began to increase from his mouth until it culminated into a full-on whimper. "What'chu mean?"

I applied more pressure; I was certain it would pop any second. This poor boy was flexible. "Give me a name of another local dealer."

"K-K-Kirby." He stuttered. I broke the finger.

"His full name?" I broke the next finger.

T-Bag no longer fought back the pain and with it came the tears, little kid tears. Drool rolled down the corner of his mouth as his pink lips curled over his teeth. He sobbed without noise now. I tapped his face to remind him I was waiting.

"Kirby Latrell." He said then let out this long high pitched *weeee* sound. T-bag's pain tolerance had reached the threshold. Soon he would be useless, and his screaming would only put me in danger. It was time to leave. I looked at him there in the corner of the room, curled up on the floor crying, holding both hands out limply. Every breath he took the pain pulsated through one finger and out the other. The mighty T-bag was no more. I punched him square in the face. His head snapped back and bounced off the wall with equal force, leaving a dent. His crying ended.

There wasn't enough time to finish searching the house and there was always the chance that girl was a loyal hoe. She could have gone straight to T-bag's employer or gathered some of his friends. It was time to leave.

Before I left, I stopped to do two things, one flush the dope and two take T-bag's cell phone.

I walked out of the apartment locking the door behind me. Once in my truck I rolled out looking both ways for the girl. She was gone into the darkness, back to Delroy and on to the next Dick. I took the vest off and stuffed it in a bag along with the suppressor. I drove out focused on what I came to do and accomplished. It wasn't over. This was just the start of something. I broke an egg tonight and no one would be making omelets out of it. T-bag will be dead because of me. I was okay with that.

The feeling that I should have killed T-bag tickled my ribs. I wanted desperately to scratch it, make it go away but I couldn't. While in jail, I wouldn't have hesitated in a fight, out now, I had to separate this war, compartmentalize it. My mission was to hurt the dope peddlers in town, I knew they wouldn't go away for good but long enough for Pope to get out of town sober. Word would spread one way or the other and an army would begin to mass. I was one man to take them on, I would need more guns.

I found my way out of the neighborhood and headed north. The night was not over, no time for sleep. There was still no plan for Pope. All my energy had been spent looking for the drug dealer who supplied him the drugs. I'm a man looking to solve problems with the easiest solution, like electricity I'm after the path with least resistance but get in my way and get burned.

The first step in Pope's rehab program was to get rid of the source of the drugs. In my mind this would prevent relapse, or at the very least make it a lot harder to relapse. I refused to think beyond the one dealer. I knew there would be more dealers that just this one T-bag, but I had to start with just one.

I drove at a steady pace catching every green light along US 1. I had the windows down enjoying the cool night air, knowing in a few hours that oppressive sun would rise and bring hell on earth. That universe I was so worried about seemed fine with me right now and I was giddy with what I had accomplished. I wanted to post it to Face Book or take a selfie with T-Bag and put it on Instagram. The craziness of that made me smile. I wanted to tell someone, not to brag but to share the excitement. I called Billy.

It rang and then he said, "Fucker better be dying." He exhaled and I could hear the cigarette smoke escape his lungs.

"Never been more alive and for the low, low price of four maybe five thousand dollars you can too, but better act in the next ten seconds."

It took a good ten seconds for Billy to respond to my upbeat attitude and coded message. "Huh? Are you high? Is this Roger Grimes, the calmest, coolest cat I know?" I could hear a slight grin in his voice, he was waking up. Our friendship had no etiquette, no boundaries, if I was happy, he was happy and the reverse. Which was usually him being happy and me faking it the best I could.

"Brother, I just stumbled upon five thousand dollars tonight. I'm not far, I can swing by and tell you all about it." We never talked business over the phone unless it was well rehearsed with a code.

"Aw, yeah I guess so. I'll meet you downstairs. The ole lady's gone to bed." He hung up. I picked up the pace.

Chapter 4

Keep your enemies closer. After tonight I'll have plenty of enemies to keep close or keep dead.

Billy Horseblood lived in Holly Hill, a working-class town stuck between a wealthier town and a famous one. Holly Hill had no beach access which kept the tax revenue down which kept a lot of other stuff down. I took residential streets to his house.

I pulled in to a 1920's Mediterranean Revival style house most people call Spanish. It was white plaster with terracotta tile on the roof. There were double doors in the front and a pair directly across the house in the back. The house was perfectly positioned to catch the breeze from the river a couple blocks over and carry it through the house. The thick interior walls kept the place cool. It was a well-designed Florida home with one major rarity, a cellar.

Billy had bought the house in foreclosure. We spent a winter completely remodeling it. He had this thing about that cellar he wouldn't let go, and after I saw the floor plans, he designed it all made sense. Back then, we were heavy into our secret line of work as thieves. I was twenty-one and just starting to get comfortable picking locks, safes and carrying a gun. Billy was in his thirties and held that master's confidence after twenty years in the business. He was at the top of his game; he knew all the best fences and got all the best tips to make a score.

When this house came on the market, he just couldn't let it go. Sitting outside a bank fifty miles inland, Billy would be talking about his plans for the place. He went on and on about remodeling the basement and putting in secret compartments throughout the house. It was so real in his mind that I was beginning to see it myself. So, when he finally laundered enough stolen cash to put down, we went to work building it out.

I swung into the driveway of Billy's place and killed the motor quick. Now in his forties, he lived in the Spanish home with a girlfriend and her terrible teenage daughter. Alley was fifteen but looked twenty. Her mother Tammy was thirty something and dressed like she was fifteen. The two of them were always at each other's' throats. Billy spent more and more of his time beneath the house. The driveway went past the house to a small wood frame garage built sometime in the 1950's. I walked past the house around to the back. A light shown on my feet, so I knew he was in the basement.

I descended red painted concrete stairs to a white wooded door with black hinges. I wrapped a couple of times and let myself in. I had to stoop while inside and move along a concrete walkway with kitchen cabinets nailed to the wall on my left and exposed sand and fill dirt to my right. Then I stepped down into the finished basement.

Billy was sitting on an old gold velvet couch he got when his grandmother died years back. He had a fresh Miller High Life can in his hand that blended into the couch perfectly. The fan was on low, humming and swirling the ever-damp basement air. Billy was dressed in a white wife beater and cutoff jean shorts. On his feet he had white socks and a pair of Jacksonville Jaguars flip-flops. His long hair was wet and out of the customary braid. Across the red shag carpet was a mini-fridge and a TV on a midcentury stereo cabinet. The record player was spinning an early Eagles album that I couldn't name, I wasn't much of a music-file.

"So, what's got Roger Grimes's dick so hard this late at night?"

"Billy, it's only twelve thirty."

Billy shrugged and stuck a cigarette in him mouth. He was settling in as a working stiff now, complete with a live-in girlfriend. The days of us crossing the country, robbing and stealing were fading into obscurity. Owning and running an automotive repair shop was more work than he expected. Being honest was hard work. I knew Billy wasn't done living life yet, he was just in a rut, and I figured getting in on it might pop him out of it.

I pulled a beer out of the fridge and sat on a tall metal stool with a car parts store logo on it. "I rolled a drug dealer tonight and took his cash." I sipped beer. Billy crinkled his brow and said nothing. Then I pulled the wads of cash out and tossed it to him. He thumbed it and put it down.

We sat in silence. I finished half the bottle before I said, "So?"

Billy grabbed another beer. He stood after bending for the beer, overarching his back, getting it to stretch. "Well, what for?" he said half in a yawn, half stretching voice.

"Dude, I made sixty-three hundred dollars tonight and you're asking what for?"

"No, you stole sixty-three hundred dollars from a drug dealer." He sat back down on the gold couch, and I watched his beer disappear. He came up for air and said, "So, Roger Grimes went legit and won't meet with Smitty, but he will roll drug dealers."

"I did it for my friend Pope. He's addicted to heroin and wanted it to stop. Smitty just wants us to steal something, something that will make someone else rich. Peanuts for us. I'm trying to make a change for a friend even if he isn't ready to do it himself." I finished my beer and left the bottle on the small counter along the wall. I could see the wheels turning in Billy's head. He was always the calculating sort. Though he never appeared intelligent, having never finished high school, he was smart. He could plan a heist, remember all the guard times and security codes, and plan escape routes without writing a thing down. His mind worked like he was in a maze running down different paths until they came to an end. He got to the end of mine quick.

"At first, I was just angry. So, I tracked down the dealer who sold to Pope. He was out at the Board Walk. Actually, it was a segregate, kid named Jimmy. He sent me to a guy named T-Bag's apartment."

"T-Bag? You went alone and trusted this kid wasn't setting you up?"

"Yeah, I don't know something about that kid seemed alright. I broke his phone to buy time. T-bag had a friend over. A young girl maybe fifteen."

"Shit, like Allie's age?" Billy sipped his beer.

"Yeah, just about."

"Did you kill him?"

"No."

"Why?"

"I don't know." I said, but the truth was I never killed anyone. Billy was never a violent man either. As far as I knew he only ever got mixed up in one shooting and no one died. Possessions, Billy always instilled, can be replaced, life cannot. It was either age or experience that had made him more conscious of the consequences we would face after each heist.

I went on to tell him what happened at the apartment, what T-bag gave up and how I got away. With a greasy thumb, Billy flipped through the bills once more. A long silver string of smoke rose from his cigarette that was mostly ash waiting to be dumped.

Billy looked up at me, "How is stealing from drug dealers any different than rich people?"

I said nothing. There was something that felt right about what I was doing, something that would help and not hurt those around me. Taking pictures of old Mr. Watson cleaning his gutters was the high of a job well done, but who did I help? A single old guy trying to get by or the insurance company making sure they got their fair share. The dial on my moral compass was spinning again with no clear direction.

"I'll help you, but tomorrow we meet with Smitty."

I hung my head.

"Look, I would love to have you by my side but this ain't your fight. You don't need to be there."

"Shit Grimes, I didn't ask your permission to join you. I owe you this." Billy sucked the last of his cigarette and smashed it out.

I just looked at him, blank faced.

"So, you want me to help you hit Delroy, right? No point in tracking down that Kirby fella."

I shook my head, "Kirby is the quickest way to Delroy. If I waste days, weeks tracking him down, he might get tipped and it's over."

Billy sat down on the couch. He looked up me with his elbows on his knees. "I just want to make sure, are you doing this for Pope or you?"

Billy was to the point. He saw me, looked in my eyes and knew better than to go off with me jacked up on adrenaline, a drug I hadn't felt in a while. We stopped bank robbing when I went to jail and stopped stealing altogether since I got out. This was my *legit life* and his too. Fifteen years of my life was on the other side of the law, and I had got away clean, no felony record. Billy had a few spots on his but was not in prison, so he was free and wanted to stay that way.

"Shit Billy, this is about more than money." I balled my fist and bounced it off my knee. This was beginning to be less about Pope and more about me. It was about a purpose. It was about giving back what I had taken.

"If this is for Pope, we take half and send him off with the other half. Maybe some nice rehab or something. If this ain't for your friend, then you and I split it fifty-fifty."

Billy went to the record player and changed it over to Metallica. His mood was changing, he was finding his old ways, getting out of the maze he was trapped in. I could feel the anticipation growing in Billy as the guitar cried battle and the drums pounded out machinegun fire. He began to pace.

Before Billy said anything a timed thudding came from up above. Tammy was up and moving around. We suspended our conversation instead turning our attention upstairs, waiting to hear a second set of thudding which would mean Alley was home and no one wanted that. A voice did break the silence, coming through the one A/C vent in the ceiling, "You smoking down there again?"

Billy stuck his face to the vent and blew all the smoke his lungs could hold. "Nah, go back to bed." Billy turned with a smile. "Okay Grimes, what's the game plan?" His blood was pumping again, and the kid gloves he was just handling me with had peeled off. It did not take anything more than Tammy simply asking what he was doing to bring him in.

Billy had brought it all back around for me. I nodded; he knew that I meant it was for Pope. The man could separate business and pleasure. When we took a job, it was all business, we never used an extra person. If the job could not be done with just the two of us, we didn't take it. Billy never talked about it, but I always assumed it was a double cross in his past that made him so exclusive.

"If it's the same Kirby I know, he's a piece of shit. He won't be missed." Billy stood up and reached into one of the built-in cabinets. He slid the back panel out and pulled and put on a pair of black and red mechanics gloves. Once on, he reached in and pulled out a revolver and a box of .357 rounds that went with it. He proceeded to wipe the piece down then pop the cylinder out and snapped it shut, reassured it was loaded. Then he grabbed a few rounds from the box and shoved them in his pocket. I was on my feet with my heart beating again at a screaming pace. I was alive.

****

Billy's shop was dark when I swung the C10 into the first bay. I sat in the dark while Billy got out and went into the office. It did not take long for him to come back with a set of keys. He jingled them with a smile and twitched his head for me to follow him. I jumped out, grabbing a gym bag with the vest and suppressor.

The shop was long and dark. I had to watch where I stepped and watch where Billy was taking me at the same time. Three of the four lifts held classic cars. The first was a '68 El Camino with a 396 ci and breather jutting from the hood. The next was a two tone 1956 Ford Coupe convertible and the final car was a black Stingray Corvette with red leather interior. The Vette looked pretty stock from the outside, the way it sat, but underneath it was all custom from the chassis to LED head lights. The dash was all custom as well with custom formed digital gauges.

Billy stood over something draped by a teal car cover. He held one corner in his hand. I waited as he whipped it back like a magician revealing the lady sawed in half. I looked at a boat on wheels. It was a faded maroon four door 1996 Impala.

"We're gonna look like cops." I sighed.

"No way. They all drive new Chargers." Billy looked at me like I was an idiot and maybe I was. I had been hopped up on adrenaline fresh from a fight and all I could think about was getting high again. Right there, there was nothing between Pope and me. I had been chasing a high since I took those pictures of Watson working on his house. The insurance company was happy, Willis Sanford was happy, and I thought I was happy. I needed to get that happy high again and it would come by beating the shit out of some drug dealer who may or may not have sold drugs to Pope. Now I dragged Billy Horseblood into this. I shook it off and got back to it.

"Okay man, tell me there's a motor swap in there." I said with faked enthusiasm.

"What's wrong with stock?" Billy smirked and pulled the rest of the teal cover off, wrapping it into a fluffy ball and setting it aside. When he was done, he looked at me and laughed, "It's a Z06 dumbass."

"Alright then." I pulled the heavy door open and plopped down on the large grey fabric seat. The inside had a smell of citrus hand cleaner and fresh rubber.

Billy cranked over the key and the beast erupted with a mean growl. He let the car idle without speaking. He grabbed the custom floor shifter and dropped it into reverse. Before I heard the squeal my head dropped as my chin touched my chest then just as fast it popped back, nearly taking my head off.

Billy cracked a red neck cackle followed with some Redman whooping to accompany the roar of the 650 horsepower as the Impala broke loose from the parking lot.

Easing off the accelerator we coasted along US 1 slowing from the eighty miles per hour we reached in a few seconds. The town was quiet, a great night to be out cruising. The clubs would be closing soon, and the drunk patrons would be leaving, figuring out where to keep the party going. The streets would be high with tension, fights and hook-ups would be going down. I hadn't been to a club in years, never cared for them. I looked for the hole in the wall places, where everyone carried a knife or a gun, not because we were bad asses but because it ensured we would be left alone.

Billy hit the window button. The poorly tinted glass whined as it rocked back and forth eventually stopping halfway down. Billy's cigarette hand pushed down on the glass, and it eventually gave in the track and subsided down the door. My window went down easy.

"Best car I ever built." Billy said watching the road. His smile was obnoxiously large. He was high, high doing the thing he loved most, driving a fast car he made fast. Hours of sweat struggle and busted knuckles was paid back by the smooth shifting seven speed tranny and beastly hum of 7.0 liters. It really was a sick sleeper, and I even broke a grin every time the Impala jumped.

"So, where we off to?" Billy lit up his second cigarette.

"To find Kirby. I looked up his record and he stay off Fairway."

"Okay. What's in the bag?"

"A vest and a suppressor." I looked out the window. "We can stop by my place and get another vest."

"Nah." Billy was being good now with the horsepower, resisting the urge to tromp it anymore.

I turned and studied his face then. It wasn't that he said no it was the way he said, like he had it covered, like he was made of ceramic plates and whatever bullets may be thrown at him tonight, they wouldn't penetrate. "Then wear that one. T-bag had a nine under his pillow. Who knows about this Kirby guy?"

He did not respond. The silence was insulting.

We drove on and then Billy looked over at me, his hand reached out to the tuner. "Ready?" and he pushed the "Play" button on the old CD player. A deep vibrating rattled everything in the car as bass from the old Woo Tang song began to thump. Billy smiled and pushed down on the gas pedal. The Impala rolled on down US 1, next, west on Fairway over the tracks and through the neighborhood no two white boys should ever be after dark.

Through the neighborhood we went in the '96 Impala and as we passed the driveways of the homes, taking this car made even more sense. Many of the cars in this neighborhood were large sedans, Impalas, Crown Vics and 300's. Other than what was under the hood, we blended nicely.

Billy knew where he was going, but we took our time. I had one butterfly in my gut that quickly turned into many. With a hard swallow, I redirected the nervous energy into a cause, a reason to be doing this and that reason was Pope. His gaunt sunken face hovered in my mind. To see such a warrior beaten down by the only enemy he could not defeat, himself, spurred me on. Tonight, I would hurt Kirby and find a new name for my list. The dope in this town was taking a hit, and I was swinging for the fences.

Billy looked over with a nod, he eased the car slowly past a white gravel drive that led to a faded blue block home. One big oak spread out with the roots thick and exposed rippled through the mostly dirt yard. The living room light shown through tattered white blinds. The small window in the door had cardboard duct taped over. There were two cars in the drive, one was on four flat tires and looked as though it hadn't been driven this decade. The other car was a black Impala, about ten years old, on 22-inch chrome rims.

"This is the place. That's his car." Billy let us pass. He took us to the next intersection and made a left then pulled off the road.

"So, what's the plan stud? Breaking in is my specialty but breaching doors, you got more experience with that."

"I got lucky with T-Bag."

"Yeah, you did, going alone halfcocked."

"I've had time to think about this. Do you know if he has dogs?"

"No, just a mean old granny, probably bites just as hard."

I had sunk back in my seat. Truth was, I hadn't thought it through. I was going in blind just as before and bringing Billy with me. The clock was ticking, and we had to either take Kirby now or wait it out until the heat I brought tonight cooled around these dealers. There was no time to delay.

"You've been in his house?" I asked formulating my plan as I went.

He shook his head no. Damn.

"Alright than," I paused for a moment. It must have been a familiar look in my eye, one Billy had seen many times while on jobs together. Whatever my expression was, Billy's expression was saying *Stop*.

"Keep the car running and pop the trunk." I hopped out. I could hear him say a few swear words, but the trunk popped as I rounded the back of the car.

The black mask was once again rolled down over my face. The Glock with the suppressor held at my right side. *Fire control, fire control* was repeated over and over in my mind as I walked up to the house. Just as with T-Bag's apartment, I felt the door and listened close. I could hear a television on. Peering between broken blinds, the flash of the television programming illuminated the room. I let myself in. In a large stuffed recliner sat an old woman with silver grey hair up in curlers. She was wrapped in a pink bath robe and had black Velcro shoes on her feet. Her hands were folded over in her lap and there was a metal cane beside the chair.

I crept past her and down the hall, looking back at her every couple of seconds. I could hear only my breath now, pushing against my black mask as it escaped my mouth. The first door I came to was on my left. No light shown below the door. I touched the knob and the door moved in freely. I peeked in and saw two kids three and five asleep on a double mattress with no sheets. Both were in diapers despite their size and judging by the smell, needed changing. I moved on.

The next door had light coming from below. I could hear the faint high pitched scrambled sound of music coming from ear buds turned all the way up. Then came the distinct sound of someone hitting a bong, the gurgling and long exhale. I moved on to the next two dark rooms. Both were empty. I went back to the door emanating light. It was time to enter.

I held my pistol close to my chest as I put a shoulder to the door. Once inside I scanned the room for movement which there was very little. In a haze of pot smoke, one man sat on the edge of his bed with his back to me. From a small flat screen on a laminate wood dresser missing a top drawer he was watching YouTube videos of people failing. He let out an over exaggerated laugh as one snow boarder collided with another.

From behind I figured he was in his twenties. He had a fade style hair cut with about two inches of hair sprouting from the top of his head. He wasn't wearing a shirt and had on only black basketball shorts. This had to be Kirby.

I wasn't taking chances. From behind I wrapped my arm around his neck and proceeded to choke him into unconsciousness. Once out, I dragged him from his room.

Billy had moved on from Wu Tang to Kenny Chesney when he caught me coming out the front door with Kirby over my shoulder. He fired up the Z06 motor and looked around. I could tell by his posture he had the .357 on his lap.

Kirby was not a large man, maybe five foot seven and 125 pounds. It was an easy fit into the trunk of the big car.

We were doing sixty miles per hour before Billy asked, "Where to?"

"Let's find a swamp."

It did not take long to be away from the city lights and out in the sticks where the gators and wild hogs finished off anything we decided to leave behind. Off the highway, Billy turned onto a white limestone dirt road. Instantly we were swallowed by the darkness, all the ambient light from the city was blocked by the tall pines and scrub oak. The wash board road rattled our teeth, so Billy was forced to keep the speed below twenty.

From the dirt road, Billy turned off down a less traveled road and twice as bumpy. It was really nothing more than a wide space between pines. Eventually small saplings blocked our path.

"There's a pond down there about a hundred yards." Billy threw the car in park and shut down the massive motor.

The forest was a live with calls and warnings from insects on the ground and in the trees. The air was still and thick with humidity, the kind that wraps around you and suddenly your clothes feel heavy as they stick to your skin. Wearing this mask was nearly unbearable.

Kirby was awake when I popped the trunk and looked down at him. I was still in my mask and Billy had his as well, and had his ponytail tucked into his shirt. There was a look in the drug dealer's eyes I did not expect, he looked pissed off. His bare foot came flying out and nearly caught me in the chin. I went in with both hands around his throat and lifted him out of the car. He dangled for a few seconds as Billy grabbed his arms, pinning them behind his back. Kirby spit at me and breathed heavy but said nothing.

Billy made quick work of zip-tying Kirby's wrists. Kirby struggled against the restraints but failed to break them. He kicked out at me, but I blocked it with my own leg. I threw a right to get his attention. He spit again and started saying, "C'mon man, c'mon. untie me and let's do this."

It was tempting but not what I kidnapped him for. If I wanted to fight, I would have fought him back in his room. Kirby had to lead me to Delroy.

"I ain't scared you rag head mother fuckers." He spit again at me so I threw a one, two. The one he almost dodged if not for Billy holding him up. There was no doubt Kirby was a fighter. His derogatory comment however, had me perplexed. I had no idea why he thought we were Middle Eastern. I did not let the questions deter my actions as I threw two quick body shots, weakening the little man's knees.

I didn't ask him questions or make any statements, I just kept throwing well placed punches. Kirby started to go limp, his breathing was labored, and one eye was completely swollen shut. Billy must have lessened his grip or it was the lubricant provided by all the sweat, which ever it was, Kirby sprang from zip ties with a flying fist.

My arms went up quick which blocked the blow, but the little guy had serious force behind it. I had let my guard down and did not have my feet planted. The shot knocked me back off balance. Kirby had another fist fly at me before I could even get my legs right. His flying left glanced off the side of my skull filling my ears with the sound of his bone on mine. The punch twisted my mask, blinding my right eye.

I got low, keeping my face covered. I felt his leg swing into my side stinging my hip and scrapping the soft side of my skin.

Billy grabbed him from behind once more and again the fiery little guy broke free. His fists were wild as he spun and swung on Billy. Billy stepped back and missed both hands coming for his face. Billy started to dance with kid who kept light on his feet in the needle covered white sand. They both juked at each other looking for that opening. Kirby was quick to spin and keep an eye on me, rightly so. Billy faked and Kirby went for it putting up his hands. I donkey kicked him right between his shoulder blades, sending him sailing forward, belly flopping into the sand.

Kirby laid flat for a moment while his lungs filled with air once more. He sat up. White sand clung to his sweaty torso contrasting in the night against his dark skin. Once he spit the last of the sand out of his mouth he looked up and said, "I'mma get you mutha fuckers."

I put the Glock in his face. "I want Delroy Antus."

Kirby's eyes were slits and his lip curled, he was caged, and the beast wanted out. "If I don't kill you, he will. He gonna kill your whole family. You stupid mutha fuckers." Then the eyes grew large in the moon light, his curled lip parted as he smiled wide.

"I've gone through this already tonight with one of your co-workers. I made him talk and I will make you talk." This one was tougher than T-Bag, it was obvious. The kid was angry, and he was allowed to be angry with us. He would be stubborn and pain resistant. Breaking bones would have little effect on his tongue. We had to threaten something he valued more than his life.

"If you won't talk to us, then maybe that old lady back at your place will."

Kirby screamed and lunged toward me, throwing sand as he flew. It took all the fire control I had not to pop Kirby right then, double tap to his chest, but I held tight. Billy was quick to grab Kirby by the hair and slam him into the ground. Next Billy's boot went over the young man's throat. He pressed down.

Kirby's eyes bulged and veins popped around his forehead as she struggled against the boot. His life was slipping away with every shortened breath. Billy smirked and pushed down. Kirby's legs kicked and his arms flailed until all went limp.

I tapped Billy's shoulder and he let off the young drug dealer. Billy pulled another zip tie from his blue jeans pocket and zipped Kirby's wrists once more. He patted the kid's head like he had been a good dog.

"You serious about going back for Granny?"

"If I have to." I said then kicked the kid in his side. He moaned and stirred, rolling in the sand and pine needles. His eyes were clenched tight. He opened them and looked up at the two of us looking down at him.

"Shit." Kirby's voice scratched out through sandpaper vocal cords.

I knelt down next to him, "I don't need to kill your granny myself. I will find Delroy with or without you. When I do, I will tell him you lead me to him. I'm sure he will kill her for me."

Kirby looked down at his bound wrists. "Pool Room next to the laundry mat on Fairview."

I stood up. Still looking down at him I said, "You're a tough kid. You have a good combo you throw but try to focus on where you're putting it. Don't get wild and keep your head, you'll be a better fighter."

I turned and walked back to the car. Billy stood next to kid not sure of what my move was and what he should be doing. This was new territory for us, kidnapping and torture. Our crimes were always committed in solitude, no witnesses. Now we had to leave one and I knew, just as I wasn't comfortable with it, he would not be either. Pope was alive, strung out and just hanging on, but so far not dead. That was the scale in which I judged these dealers. Billy would need to know this.

Billy stood with me at the car. In a whispered tone he said, "Hey man, what are we gonna do with him?"

"Leave him."

"He'll make it outta here in the morning, it's not that far from the main road."

"I'm not killing him, and we have nowhere to stash him. We just have to stay fast and get Delroy tonight."

"Shit Grimes, this is cutting it close. Since when you leave no room for error?"

"Since I started busting drug dealers." I got in the car. I heard Kirby yell something and turned to see Billy standing there looking at the young dealer. From the small of his back, I saw the unmistakable shape of the .357 pistol grip. His hand went up to his waist but stopped short. I reached for the door handle and got in. Billy swung his pointed cowboy boot into Kirby's face.

Billy settled in behind the wheel of the Impala. He said nothing as he started the car and backed it all the way out, down the dark sandy road to the main dirt road we came in on.

"My office." Was all I said. Billy nodded and drove on in silence.

Billy followed me into the office door. I didn't bother turning on a light and found Pope still asleep on the couch.

There was a water bottle out, so he had got up at some point and grabbed some water. Then I saw the bucket he vomited in.

There was still more work to do, and I had to do it fast. Billy paced around with nowhere to sit. He leaned against the wet bar with his arms crossed and his head down.

My desk chair squealed as I leaned back. The glow of the computer gave my face a blue hue and cast a black silhouette against the large office window behind me. Sanford set me up with a password to LexisNexis. My instructions were to only use it on cases he assigned me. Delory Antus was out there and so was the word on the street. Creeping ever closer, jumping from shadow to shadow. From T-Bag's lips to the Delroy's ears, we were coming.

Delroy was ugly. In one of the mug shots, he had two gold teeth, and his head was clean shaved. A tattoo on the left side of his face spelled out *juddment*, yes, *juddment* either the tattoo artist got it wrong, or he did when he told the artist what he wanted. His big head went right into broad shoulders with no mention of a neck except a dark bulging ring just above his tight collar.

Some men are born unlucky. Not poor, not dumb, just unlucky. This was Delroy. He was unlucky because of his face. It was the face of a man that evoked enough rage in the average person to punch it. I was feeling that need, I wanted at this guy regardless of the crime. Poor, unlucky Delroy.

I studied the partial grin, the deep-set eyes, and the scar on his cheek. A rumbling started in my gut. It was not hunger or nerves but anticipation. I could feel a fight coming. It was that same feeling I had in high school when the young 3rd Street boys tried me, and it was that same gut rumbling that carried me through every confrontation since.

I read over the rap sheet, just a list of things he was caught doing, no way to find out the things he didn't get caught for. It was a wide range from simple shop lifting to assault, to attempted murder. Delroy's last known address was not far. The chance he was there was far though. I handed the tablet to Billy. His eyes scanned the open documents then handed the tablet back to me.

"How much did you get off Kirby?" Billy said flatly.

"Nothing. I took him out so fast, I didn't grab anything."

"What?"

"Sorry man. You can have the half I took from T-bag. Take it all, I don't care."

"Shit Grimes. You're getting too emotional about this job; you know that's trouble." Billy went to the bar and poured some bourbon into a glass.

"Yeah, I 'm emotional, this whole thing is about balancing the scales for Pope, getting him clean and out of this shithole. The money was just bonus and salt in the bad guys' wounds." My eyes fell on the sleeping man.

Billy sipped the bourbon and then said, "Take your eye off the money and it all goes to shit, man. All the jobs we pulled, any of them ever about anything else besides the money?" His voice was getting louder, and I didn't want Pope to wake, he'd have questions and he wouldn't accept the answers. We were almost through this, only a couple more hours.

"We're fucking robbers Billy, it's only ever about the money." I agreed but wasn't following him.

"Right. We're robbers Grimes. We steal money, we're not avenging angels. If we stay focused on stealing money, we can pull this off. If we go into Delroy's hood and think we're gonna change lives you're wrong and probably dead." He kicked back the rest of the bourbon in one gulp then said, "So what's it gonna be?"

Billy was right, I was going about this all wrong. So far, I survived on pure luck, luck they were home and luck they were alone. Delroy would be neither of those things. Pulling a bank job or cracking a safe was what we did, and we planned every step and rehearsed every step. This was off the cuff, putting us out of our element.

"The longer we wait the more likely word gets to Delroy about what we've done. He'll either gather reinforcements or go into hiding." I grabbed the bottle of Kentucky Bourbon and poured my own glass. I sipped it and let it burn the back of my throat. Billy moved on to his second glass. Pope rolled on the couch but didn't wake up.

"Well," Billy began, "seems we have no choice on when we go but how we go we can do something about. Remember the Winter Park job a few years back? The one we split up and took two cars?"

I nodded.

"You go in first, take your truck. I'll be nearby, make a couple of passes until you go in. Then wait for me before you start breaking people's faces. I'll be coming in from the back door."

I smiled, "Okay. Say, when was the last time you picked a lock?"

"Shit." Billy didn't say anything after that, just nudged me getting me moving. I left Pope there once more and headed out into the heart of 3rd Street territory.

We split up at the shop. I took my C10 and rumbled towards the Pool Hall. I still had the long sleeve shirt on which was perfect timing for my A/C to go out. I would have to charge it later but there are a lot of other fixes I needed to do to the truck first. Being broke for the last few months I let things slide and it was beginning to show. Daytona, for all that it is, is a car town above all else. Your ride in this town means something. The changes in my life were for the better and some of those would include my truck. Now as I drove towards a fight, all that I built was on shifting sand.

When you're out in the field, especially alone, you learn to trust your gut. Buried down deep a small little twinge takes hold of your spine and climbs up into your brain telling you what to do and where to go. That twinge saved my life more than once. I trusted it. Right now, it leads me a couple of extra blocks out of the way back to the office. I drove east on North Street and slowed as I passed a small three store strip mall. One end was 24-hour laundry mat, next a convenient store and on the other end a pool hall with a sign that said it was still open. Passing by I spotted it, gold 24-inch rims on a black Infiniti. I pulled in.

I quieted the rumble from the LS1 under the hood of my C-10 and sat in the corner of the parking lot watching, waiting, for something, anything to happen. Through the large pane window, a woman moved clean laundry from one of the washers to the dryer. She eyeballed me for a second but kept about her business. In front of the pool hall a couple of guys exited but remained near the door. One struck up a blunt and both men took turns hitting it.

Both men were in long sleeve baggy shirts and saggy pants that tapered down tight around the spotless raw hide yellow work boots. The taller of the two had a black do-rag on and the other a black ball cap with a flat bill cocked to the side. Both were engaged in light chatter with the occasional chuckle. Might have just been what they were smoking. I needed to get closer, get past them and inside.

Under my seat I had a grease-stained t-shirt I used to check my oil. In the glove box were brass knuckles. I shoved them in my pocket with the black mask. That should be enough to get me past them without suspicion, though there was nothing I could do about my skin color.

I slipped out of my truck and scurried to the corner of the building. Covered by shadow, I knelt and grabbed a handful of dirt. I rubbed it into my feet and hands. Next, I gouged my eyes to get the red and watery. Then came back around the corner to the front of the strip. I walked under the bright florescent lights of the laundry mat and past the closed convenient store. As I neared the two, I began to limp, dragging my right foot, scraping it along the sidewalk. The two men stopped talking and stared.

The tall one with heavy eye lids covering red eyes flicked his chin up at me and tapped his friend on the shoulder. The other, in the ball cap, was already looking at me. I continued towards them dragging my foot.

"Yo, I think you in the wrong hood cuz." The tall one said. His breath smelled like burnt rubber and his teeth were black along the gums.

I propped up a smile and mumbled to myself as I hobbled past them. I could hear Billy's Impala rumble by. The two door men paid the car no attention, as they paid me no attention. Their focus was on their conversation. Once I was past them, I was out of their mind. That's when I rolled the mask down over my face.

They weren't going to let me in so I would have to let myself in. I spun around and cold cocked the tall one with the knuckles. He dropped quickly and sprawled out on his back. His head hung off the curb and his eyes rolled back into their sockets. He wasn't getting up anytime soon. The little one went for something in his waist band.

He struggled to pull the pistol clear. I kicked out with my foot, knocking the gun to the ground. Next, I got in close and stepped on his baggy pant leg, dropping his pants around his ankles. He was smart and kept his hands up. I stepped back and left my hands down, baiting him to come at me. He made small steps and kept his hands moving. He mumbled some nasty words, but I didn't let it bother me. He was just a steppingstone to my prize, Delroy.

I threw a left jab, he was quick to lean back and countered with a one, three. I blocked the first one and ducked the three. The missed hook exposed his side, and I took him there. I jammed my right as far as I could under his ribs until I heard them crunch. He gasped in pain, and I hit him again. He stumbled back holding his side trying hard to breath shallowly.

Two white moon shaped eyes looked up at me. I spun, kicking him in the side of the neck. He hit the pavement. I went and checked on the big guy. He was breathing but still out. I dragged them both off to some bushes on the side of the parking lot. On my way back to the pool hall entrance I picked up the little one's pistol and checked the wheel to see it was loaded. It was a Smith & Wesson thirty-eight revolver that fit well in my pocket. The mask, I rolled up on my head like a ski cap. It was time to go in.

Inside, the place was dimly light, mostly by neon beer signs shining through a haze of smoke. To my left was a bar with stools bolted to a black and white checkered linoleum floor. The bar tender was a heavy guy with a sparse beard made up of little black pigtail hairs and a toothpick between two fat lips. His fat fingers held a pint glass and white dish rag. He stared at me, never taking his eyes off me. I kept my hands up on my head scratching randomly and trying to keep my face covered as I looked around. To the right were two rows of pool tables. Beyond that were five booths. Two men occupied the corner booth. They looked relaxed until realizing I was standing there.

At the bar I took a seat and ordered a beer. The bartender didn't bother to move anything but his large hands wiping the pint glass. I pulled out five twenty-dollar bills and put one on the bar. That brought a smile to the bartender's face. He put the pint glass down and reached below the bar. My heart rate picked up as I dropped my right hand closer to my waist and the grip of my Glock. His hand produced a red plastic cup filled with mostly foam and took the twenty. There was no change.

"Closing time drunk. Take it and go." The bartender said between his big lips. Up close I could hear his labored breathing.

"I'll drink it here. I'm meeting someone." I sipped through the foam, tipping the cup far back to reach actual beer. The bartender put both his large mitts on the bar and leaned forward. I could feel his moist breath and smelled his last meal of fried fish.

"Pssst, hey." He whispered. "I said get out!" he bellowed. The two in the back got up and made their way towards me. The bartender put a hand up halting their advance. His eyes were on me as he spoke to the men, "Go out front and get Lamont."

One of the two men was dressed in a long red tee shirt the other was wearing a wife beater. Both men were lean and had on baggy jeans. The red shirt walked past me slowly. He got to the door and put his hand on it. I stood up with my beer and took a couple steps his way. As he pushed the door open, I moved quickly and put a shoulder to the red shirt. He went through and stumbled into the empty parking lot. I shut the door and locked it. Then I spun on my toes to see the wife beater headed my way.

His hands went out backed by a snarl on his face. Mine was meaner. We collided, hard. His grip was tight just above my elbows, and he rocked me side to side. His height gave him leverage so I had to take that way. I pushed his arms up and out then shot in. My arms wrapped around his thin waist as I twisted and lifted, slamming him down on the checkered floor. He lay sprawled out like a smashed spider.

I scrambled up his back to his face and proceeded to pummel it into the dirty linoleum. I only had seconds before big boy behind the bar grabbed for something. I sprang like a startled cat just as the shotgun went off, disseminating the wife beater's back, blowing chunks of flesh and plasma my way. I rolled behind a pool table and wiped my face. The shotgun went off again.

I jetted out from behind the table, staying low. The big man had stepped around from behind the bar. I leveled the Glock and sent two rounds his way. His knees buckled. He flailed back, arms raised above his head, and crashed into the mirrored shelves behind him. They broke against his weight sending bottles of liquor cascading to the floor. His arms were not strong enough to hold his weight on the bar. A bullet had ripped through each leg, the muscle split and spilled blood, they could not hold him. He fell face first into the bar and eventually the floor.

The guy in the wife beater was slowly getting on all fours. I kicked him in the face. His jaw snapping as my shoe impacted the bone. He sprawled out on the floor.

The red shirt was still banging on the front door, but that wasn't the door I was worried about. From the back of the room a door flew open, and two men dressed in black came through simultaneously. Their guns were up and firing. I dove to the ground and crawled between the pool tables. I laid out in the prone position and fired from under the table. Bullets caught each of them in the legs, dropping them to the floor.

One man dropped his gun immediately and tended to his legs. The other still had fight left in him and fired in my direction until he emptied the magazine. I rolled out and scrambled to the end of the pool tables. I sprang up on the table and grabbed a cue stick as I went. The thick end cracked off each of their heads. The fight in them was gone.

Moans and gun smoke filled the room. All the men, for now, were alive. I managed my shots clearly and concisely, keeping them from vital organs. This was against all my previous training. The new me, the non-criminal, wasn't going to kill these small-time gangbangers over drugs. I saw firsthand what havoc the drugs had caused in my friend's life, and I know how it does in others as well, but in the end, it was Pope's choice to shoot up. Though a poor choice, still one that he made on his own. I couldn't justify killing over it, as bad as I wanted to.

Nearing the back door, the pot smoke grew heavier. My eyes watered as I choked back the tickle in my throat. I was sweating now and felt it run down my back. Either I was going through that door, or someone was coming out. When all this started it was to help a friend. When I made a few bucks, it started being about me and I was too far in to quit now. Soon 3rd Street's drug ring would have taken a severe blow and my battle buddy would have a fresh start. I just need to make it out alive.

The high-pitched screech of worn-out desk chair wheels came from behind the door, then a voice, "Coming out brother," it was a heavy voice, it was Billy. The knob turned and the door opened. In the door was Delroy tied to a desk chair. He was angry as hell, foaming from the mouth and uttering cuss words. He had two white tube socks tied together around his head to make a blindfold and had blood soaking in above his left eye. I noticed he was barefoot as well. Billy was standing behind him with his .357 out and from what I could tell behind his black mask, a smile.

"You did this?" I said looking down at my prize. Delroy was not wearing a shirt and had on only basketball shorts. He had a muscular build, and his skin was covered in tattoos, mostly things written in script. I didn't bother to read any of it, it was all probably bull shit. Gangsters like to think they are poets or that they can't be judged and scribbling it on their skin amounts to nothing but sob stories. If your best friend got killed while running the streets then leave, start over. Trust me when I say, criminals know the cost.

"Yep," Billy walked towards the bar, "I need a drink." When he got behind the bar, he looked down at the fat bartender, stepped over him and poured some vodka over ice and added some Sprite. He rolled his mask up over his mouth and sipped it in exaggerated fashion and made his way back over to the two of us. I hadn't moved. I had my eyes on Delroy.

"Delroy." I said and his head swiveled side to side as he tried to figure out if he knew my voice. I added, "You don't know me."

"I'm gonna kill you though, I can guarantee that." He lifted his chin defiantly.

"Until then, I'm going to make sure you don't sell drugs in this town."

I looked at Billy and signaled for him to keep his eyes on the drug kingpin. I went to the back office. My mission was to do as much damage to the drugs coming into this town as I could. Something told me Delroy was not a direct importer of heroin. His reputation on the street was that of a tough guy, not to be messed with and certainly to be tied to a chair and robbed, but that is what I was doing. I was hoping for two things in that office; one, leads on who is bringing the drugs in and two, cash for Billy. After not bagging a dime from Kirby, Billy was due a cut.

I paused before heading down the hallway to put on a pair of latex gloves. Above to guide me was one bright florescent bulb with no shade. It nearly blinded me it was so bright. One wall was painted neon green and the other black. The rubber soles of my shoes pealed from the linoleum with each step and the smell of mold filled my nostrils. At the end of the hall was the office door. I stood there for a second, believing my friend had secured the room ahead of me. I kicked the door open.

Inside the office was much larger than I thought. In front of me was a black leather couch and matching love seat. A glass coffee table was settled on top of a fancy looking shaggy red rug. The large mirror behind it caught me off guard as I stared down a man in a mask with a gun. Recognizing him as myself, I moved on. To my left the room continued, long and narrow. At the end was a desk but before that lay a tiger rug. Against one wall was a massive TV, on the other a well-stocked bar. There were two leather chairs in front of the desk. The desk itself was large with papers and cash stacked on it. I fanned a stack of bills. It felt to be ten thousand dollars. I grabbed all five stacks.

Holding the cash in my hands I realized one important oversight, both planning the job but in the reasoning behind it. I never brought a bag to stow the cash. Entering a contemplative state was the last thing I wanted to do on a job. Breaking all my rules was tonight's theme. I stood there thinking about why I had not taken a brief case or bag with me. Had I not really anticipated taking cash? Did I lie to Billy about why I was so amped to take on this job? Shit. Billy was still out there keeping my ass safe while I took the loot. I had to make it right for him too, not just Pope.

On the floor near the desk was a black backpack. I searched and it was empty except traces of pot and rolling papers. I shoved the cash into the bag.

Opening all four drawers I found two handguns and another stack of cash. I took the cash. The computer monitor on the desk was off. I moved the mouse around and the screen came up. I clicked on the file folder and began sifting through the files. Each file was named after a classic or high-end car. I clicked on Maybach.

The Maybach folder was filled with Excel spread sheets. Each sheet had tabs labeled "in" and "out" and a tab that was filled with dates. There were numbers in every column that made little sense to me. The numbers didn't seem like dollar amounts or weights. The numbers were accompanied by a "f" or "m" along with alternating letters, w,b,c,m. The numbers ranged from 12 to 33 with a few random higher than 33. There were names, code names by the look of it. This spreadsheet could lead me right up the drug chain if I could figure it out. I didn't want to leave a digital trace so sending it out in an email was out of the question. My only recourse was to take a picture with my phone.

As I snapped away, a *CRACK* came from out in the hall, as the side door slammed shut. I hurried to the door of the office and waited. Billy yelled out, "Partner!"

"Good." I shouted, looked around then said, "I'm moving." as I entered the hall. The Glock was out in front but close to my chest. I slowly pushed open the side door. Beyond was a dark alley with tropical trees and palms blocking out any light fading to total darkness. In the blackness I heard the clanking of a chain-link fence being scaled. The runner didn't concern me as much as finding where the runner came from. I went back inside the pool hall, locking the door behind me.

In the main hall, Billy had his pistol up covering an open door to the john. Delroy was still tied and had a smirk on his face letting me know he knew something I didn't. What we both knew was that I overlooked a deadly mistake.

"Partner, I never saw the door. Caught a glimpse of someone run into the hall and then I yelled for you." Billy kept his eyes fixed.

I moved up to the door. The light was on inside. The gun led the way as I entered.

The bathroom had the same old checkered white and black floor. The fluorescent light above flickered as I scanned over the four-stall room. The sinks were dirty and not used often enough. The doors to the first two stalls were open and clear. In the third stall I spotted a pair of ankles wrapped in a pair of brown slacks. The shoes were leather and shiny. The belt was leather as well. As a pair of hands dipped below and clutched the pants I called out, "Don't move."

The hands let go.

"Keep 'em so I can see them." I commanded and the hands obeyed. Then I said, "Lay on the ground." I checked over the room with a few looks as I moved cautiously to the stall.

The man who laid down was white with thinning brown hair and looked to be about forty. He wore glasses and a white button up shirt that was now soaked through with sweat. The sleeves were rolled up and he laid his hands out to his sides. The door of the third stall was covered in black marker. Pictures fit for a Hustler cartoon covered most of the "Out of Order" letters.

The door to the fourth stall was open. I looked in. The purpose of the holes in the partition were obvious. The door to the stall had a regular knob and multiple locks that bolted the door shut. The toilet was removed and capped. There was a chair with a towel over it and bathmat on the floor.

I had never seen a glory hole before, not in all my travels, nothing quite like this. I'm not sure how long I stood there reading the words and phrases scribbled on the walls when I heard the man on the floor begin to cry.

With the pistol trained on him, I said, "Crawl out." He slid across the mold and mildew, under the stall door and laid flat on the floor near the sinks. His cheek was pressed against the floor, his mouth opens in a silent whine as tears rolled from his eyes and mixed with all the other fluids already on the floor. His body jerked as he fought back the whales of shame after being caught, pants down, in a men's room.

"Who are you?"

"P-p-please don't kill me." The man began to whimper in a pitch that hurt my ears. His face was a deep pink and his eyes pinched shut. He was pathetic and knew it. I felt nothing for him. Shooting him would mean nothing to me, so I let him live with his shame.

"Get up."

He went for his pants as he got on all fours.

His neck strained as he contorted to get a look at me. Watery brown eyes glazed in disbelief. Seeing my mask sent him into another whine. When I remained still, he began to move again, slowly making his way to his feet. After buckling his belt, I patted him down. Just a cellphone, keys, and wallet. He wiped his tears as I went through his wallet. There wasn't any cash. I tossed it on the counter along with the other items.

His name was Randall Brume. He was average height and weighted around 200 pounds. His peach flesh was soft and doughy. I began to hate him for being there, for making me take my time and deal with him. Now he was one more witness, one more opportunity to pick me out of a line up.

"What are you doing here?" I grunted from beneath my black cotton mask. I could feel the sweat begin to build around my eyes and I desperately wanted to rub it away.

He said nothing, just looked over at the glory hole I dragged him from. Then he looked back at me. "You can take the wallet. I swear I won't call the cops if you let me go."

"Who was in the other stall?"

Randy looked back at the stall once again. "I-I-I don't know. I mean I hope a gorgeous girl. She said she was legal." He started to smile then remembered why he had been standing in the middle of the bathroom with his pants down. The nerves kicked in and his eyes grew large as he searched mine. "Really I never saw her."

I could see the fear turn to regret in his eyes. Though he was in dress pants and a button up, I could tell they were cheap if not second hand. He needed a haircut, and his socks didn't match. Sweat beaded along his receding hairline and he kept licking his lips. His breathing was shallow and from where I was his stale breath filled my nostrils. Resorting to paying for sex was all this guy had and he didn't even know who or what was on the other side. I guess it didn't matter to him. At one time he had it together, was a professional with a life. Now life had beaten him down to this.

"Okay go out the back door," I said.

Randy didn't move. I nodded at his possessions on the counter. He scooped them up and walked quickly out. I heard the back door open and close. Billy called out once more.

"I'm good." I shouted and made my way for the main pool hall.

Billy hadn't moved. His eyes darted a little faster and he kept shifting his weight around, going from one skinny leg to the next. This was taking a while and we weren't used to taking a while. Only the overnight safe cracking jobs took time with no witnesses. Most of the jobs were quick ones, boosting a car or a bank job and neither took more than a few minutes.

I dragged him into something he never wanted. He was a cool cat and no one else in the room knew he was getting anxious but me and that was from our years of high stress jobs together. When Billy caught sight of me wearing a backpack he loosened up, the payout was coming.

Delroy sat relaxed like he was watching a couple of his boys shoot pool while he sipped on grape vodka. I hated him for it, for the pain he caused my friend and the life he ruined, ruining Delroy's life became my objective.

Billy covered the door while I looked down on the drug dealer.

"Your dope days are finished. If I trace any shit back to you, I will kill you."

"Man, fuck off." There was no fear in his eyes, none. I wanted to pull the trigger then and take him out of this world for good. "This about dope? Man, take it, I don't care. I got a new game so go on wit'ch yo self. See we all movin' up. You think this ends here? I got news for'ya, It's gonna get a whole lot worse."

There was nothing I could do with a man who did not fear me. No threat or action would change much of anything. Since I imposed a no kill policy, I could only take this so far. Between his arrogant words lay something of value, something I could steal from him to make him hurt.

So, I shot up the pool tables and lit the bar on fire.

Flickering orange flame reflected in Delroy's eyes. Smoke reached the sprinkler system and we all got wet. The rain came down soaking into my mask and clothes. The two sleeping in the back began to stir from the comas I put them in as water brought them back to life. There was no point in standing around. The flames over the bar diminished and so did my rage. I signaled to Billy, and we headed for the back door.

I paused, "I'm going to be back for you, you know that." Then I turned and ran off into the dark.

I didn't speed until I turned north up Beach Street, then I mashed the pedal and put the V8 to work, throwing me back into the bench seat with every gear change. I didn't drive straight to Billy's shop either, just covering my ass in case of a tail. It was the paranoid thief in me that kept me circling one more block. Stealing from criminals was new territory, something Billy and I had never talked about or even thought about. There was no doubt they would be looking for us. 3rd Street would not just roll over and take that hit no matter how small a loss. The next few weeks would be time to lay low, drink at home and keep the blinds closed. Pope would have his money and a bus ticket north. Billy would do like me and just hang around the shop.

Once confident there was no tail, I went to the shop.

The streetlights above Ridgewood Avenue covered the shop in an umbrella of yellow light. Beyond the edge pure blackness. All the bay doors were down and there was no light showing from the office window. I rolled behind the shop and saw nothing out of the ordinary. I shut the truck down and waited.

As I adjusted myself in the seat, a light from the office flicked on and off. That was the signal he was already in there. I grabbed the backpack and made my way in.

My hand was in my pocket gripping the Glock. As I came into the dark office my eyes quickly adjusted to make the outline of Billy sitting behind his desk with the .357 pointed at my guts. He lowered it and thumbed the hammer forward into place. I tossed the bag on the desk. We could relax, but there was no celebrating.

The office air was thick and didn't help to dry the sweat from my body. Billy remained quiet, as I took a seat. His silence told me what I already knew; this was a sloppy operation with only chump change for pay. Intrinsic good vibes didn't fit our work model. Billy is about tangibles. He is a coin to me. Heads, the side that plans a job, executes it and then leaves no trace. A dozen bank jobs and many more jewelry and antique heists. We had been shot at and chased but always got away clean, all due to Billy's ability to plan and execute. Tails, the other side was my best friend, the guy who always had my back and made sacrifices for me to succeed. He trained me up and kept me out of usual teenage trouble to teach me the trade, the art of stealing.

Tonight, I repaid that loyalty with lack of planning, exhibiting a total deficiency in what he spent years teaching me. The money I stole tonight wouldn't be enough, I'm not sure there was a dollar figure that would make Billy happy with me. The man lived by his own code. Since I was just a punk kid, I've tried copying his code, he told me every man must make his own. I'm still working mine out.

The silence was penetrating. The banned cash spilled from the bag. The thin green bricks hit the oil-stained calendar covering the top of the desk. Still Billy did not move. I began peeling off the bans and putting the bills in numerical sequence. I went to a cash counter he had and began dropping the bills through.

After a few minutes, I looked down at thirteen thousand dollars. I had overestimated the stacks and what denominations lay between the top and bottom ones.

I stood looking at Billy, "With the six I got earlier that makes nineteen grand."

He pulled the cigarette from his lips and let out long trail of smoke then he said, "Yup."

"I'm taking out ninety-five hundred for Pope. You can just keep the rest." From the smaller stacks, I made two thick ones. I took one and stuffed it in the black backpack. I left the other there on the counter.

"Okay then," I said and swung the pack over one shoulder. I waited for a dramatic reply. I wanted the speech, the lesson, the teachable moment that would come from the wise thief. Like the old days, I'd fuck up and Billy would take me out some place desolate, and after convincing me he wasn't going to kill me, he would walk me through the robbery and what went wrong where I could improve.

Cheap homemade tattoos ran up one red skinned arm, stringy long black hair and a sparse patch of stubble made up Billy's *Florida-man* look. People saw the grease under his nails or the holes in his jeans and assumed too much.

The thing is they were home asleep in their beds while Billy really shined. When he took care to scrub his hands and nails, neatly braid his hair and tuck it up under a cap. They never saw the brain that made a full proof plan to steal their money while they slept. Billy was on a different level when he planned and executed a job, a level most people will never achieve professionally.

I had failed tonight.

"Take your cut Grimes." He didn't move from his chair.

I reverted to a seventeen-year-old kid and did what I was told. The angst came with it. There was no doubt in my mind and body that I could take Billy any time, anyway, but respect had been earned. The filthy money was before me. I took half the stack without arguing. I finally stopped messing up tonight.

I opened my office door slowly and kept the light off. I could see clearly enough from the streetlights below. The chair squeaked as I sat down slowly. My mind was exhausted, and I knew after the night I had, I could sleep for days.

Pope looked comfortable curled up on the couch. He had an old Mexican woven wool blanket on him. As my eyes adjusted fully to the darkness and my hearing overcompensated for the lack of sight, I noticed the soggy pillowcase beneath his head and sweat beads across his furrowed brow. Despite the warm wool blanket, he was consumed with shivers. The pungent acid hit my back of my nose as my eyes fell on the office wastepaper basket next to the couch. Upchuck. Detox.

There was a chance Pope wouldn't be getting out of town right away. There was a dark street ahead for him. The venom was drying up turning his brain to toast and he needed desperately to calm the screaming nerves.

He would be up soon, and I could slip him the money and get him the hell out of this town. It would be enough.

My eye lids grew too heavy to bare. My head bobbed, searching for a place to rest. I guess I hadn't thought Pope staying here all the way through. He was nestled on my couch; I would have to sleep sitting up. Before I could pick a place to stretch out, everything went dark.

Chapter 5

There beneath the pocked skin and scabs was a brokenness that I could not fix. A good meal and positive talking could not fix for Pope. He had lost it all, his whole being had been freely enslaved for the puncture of a needle.

The sun burst through the office window and heated my face. My neck was stiff having been bent back making it painful to lift my sagging head. I rolled my head a few times to get things loose. I dropped my leg off the side of the desk, it was still asleep and when I stood the pins and needles attacked. After twisting my waist and bringing my arms back to stretch I dropped and did my usual routine of pushups and sit-ups.

Pope was up before me. He sat staring out at sun beaming through the large office window. The sky to the east was hazy with humidity. It was going to be a hot humid day, perfect for staying inside.

"Sleep alright?" I said as I went to the counter to make coffee.

"Yep." Pope said with a stretch, his arms going out over his shoulders.

"Good." I didn't know what else to say. Explaining the money and where it came from had not been worked out in my mind. My one-man army destroying the heroin trade in Daytona began in the heat of rage. Suddenly Pope's feelings and concerns on that hit me.

The coffee pot gurgled and hissed breaking the silence of the office. I got up and poured a cup. I said nothing as I raised another mug to Pope who nodded. I filled it and gave it to him.

"Tastes good." Pope said. We returned to silence after that. Sounds from the street, businesses opening and cars filling traffic lanes echoed up into the office.

I kept my eyes on the bag. Just as I reached for it, Pope spoke again, "I'm barely holding it together today man."

"Tough it out, you can beat this. You've won every other battle in your life." I stood up and slapped his shoulder. He looked up and gave me a half smile, there was pain in the other half. His face was flushed and sweating. He put the coffee down after only one sip.

"I think I'm going to be sick." Pope held his stomach as he rushed past me. He didn't bother to close the office door as he hurried down the hall.

I followed him to the hallway and stood there with a few of the other worker bees from the other offices, listening to the heaving sounds resonate down the marble tiled hallway. With each gut-wrenching toss, the workers dispersed back to their cubicles with emails waiting to be sent. I said nothing, there was nothing to explain to these people, if they didn't like it, they could leave.

Waiting in the office, I took the backpack out and laid the cash on the table. I thought it would help his cravings and withdrawal knowing the cash would cover one less worry. Pope staggered through the door. He sat on the couch and just stared for a moment. His eyes drifted towards me and the desk with the cash.

"What's that?" Pope said raising a shaky finger.

"Get out of town money." I smiled, "On one condition. You use it to get out of here and get help. I was thinking we can -"

Pope jumped up, not out of excitement or gratitude, but out of rage. "Is this some kinda joke. You think I haven't already tried all that? It's why I came to you Grimes, to fix me. Not throw money at me with a douche smile." Sweat beaded all over his body. He wiped his forehead and then wiped his hand on his shorts. I noticed the puke splatter on the shirt I gave him.

"I can't fix you Pope; you have to do that." I sat down. He continued to breath heavy. He paced a little then sat down all the while staring at the money.

"I'll just go buy with that."

"Not today, and hopefully not ever." I tossed a stack of cash to him.

He smirked, "Yeah, what makes you so damn sure?"

"I just am." I tossed the other stack at him. He flipped through the bills, not counting, just feeling the tiny breeze it generated.

"What'd you do, take out the drug trade in Daytona?" He said without looking at me. When I didn't reply he looked over at me. His face was wrinkled as the bills he held. "Say you didn't, say it fucker."

"C'mon Pope. I used to be a criminal, not an idiot."

"Shit man this ain't funny. You know what would happen to us, to me, if it got out that..." He tossed the cash on the couch and crossed the room distancing himself from the blood money. Paranoia seeped into his veins, 3rd Street would know it was him, they would be after him for revenge. He paced again, scratching at every sore that was finally on the mend. The brown crusty scabs were scrapped away leaving pink flesh to turn red with blood. As he dragged his fingers along his arms so came the blood streaks.

"Whoa," I said getting out of my chair, "Calm down man, take a seat. Just relax. It's cool." My arms were spread as I coaxed him back to the couch. His sweating was subsiding and so was the scratching.

"Listen," I said standing over him, "Spend the cash somewhere you can get help, just don't do it here. There's something in the water here that makes people do stupid things. Don't look back."

Pope began breathing easier. He went back to fanning the cash and smiled. "Yeah, I can do that. Thanks man."

I went back to my desk and together we searched bus fair and got him a ticket out of town. After that, knowing at four o'clock today he would be headed to Charlotte to his cousin's house, I could relax and enjoy a few hours of just shooting the shit like old times. The hours ticked by, I offered to get us some chow. Pope nodded that he could eat or would at least try. So, I headed down the block to Cooper's.

Inside Cooper's were a couple of familiar servers. The blonde who swore she knew me wasn't working. I managed to beat the lunch rush, so it didn't take long.

Back at the office I found Pope up walking around my office. He settled behind my desk as I dropped the burgers. He had on a smile that I knew was pure and of his own will.

I sat watching Pope watch his burger, like a coiled cobra and the charmer all out of charm. He didn't know if he had it in him to eat. I wanted to let him go first, but today I could no longer show restraint, I dug in. It didn't take long to finish the ten-ounce burger.

Pope was still picking at his food, pretending to have an appetite. I flopped on the old couch and kicked off my Vans. With maybe three hours of sleep in three days and with Pope's withdrawals I needed to just have the silence of an empty mind. Two minutes went by before I moved, not even sure I even blinked. My heart rate was slow, and I was calm. My mind drifted, bouncing around to memories of Pope and that life I tried to lead on the straight and narrow. It had been nothing but crooked since. Then after nearly a year in jail, I once again looked for the straight path with a state approved license in my pocket. Somehow being legitimate felt dirtier than stealing cars or jewelry. Now I'm balancing on the fence, that line when crossed, makes me either a hero or villain. I chose hero and fell into a black stillness of peace.

I sat straight up like a bolt of electricity had just brought me back from the dead. A tingle electrified every nerve, the room was still, too still. Pope was not at my desk. I hoped he was in the bathroom, but that hope disappeared when I saw the note on the desk. Damn.

I should have woke you to say good bye. I can't thank you enough man for what you have done. I really had nowhere to turn and I wasn't sure you would be there for me after the way we parted. You keep your word and that means more than anything. I think I will be alright now, starting to feel like myself again.

I'll contact you when I get settled which wont be around here.

Pope signed his name.

The money was gone. Pope would survive this, he had survived so much in his short life, and drugs would not take it now. Going after him would mean I didn't have faith in him, that I thought he was weak. I didn't do this for a pat on the back or handshake. I did it for the hope that he's sitting on a bench with his bus ticket thinking about his new life in Charlotte. It was a good scene that played through my thoughts, better than the ones of how I got the money to get him there. Putting my P.I. license on the line was all worth it now.

What good did the license do me, or my friend? In the end it was going back to what I know, how I was raised that got Pope sober and money to start over. Perhaps I didn't even have to go out and do all that. There was a feeling of being played, but not by Pope, by myself. Because I carry a gun and can fight, I went off like a superhero to save my friend's life and all he really needed was clean clothes and place to sleep safe a few nights. I went back on my own word and jeopardized everything new I had begun. That compass I carried was spinning faster now. Doing bad with good reason was screwing things up.

Ways to find Pope danced in my mind for a short time, but none of them panned out. So, I shut my eyes just for a second.

As I pulled myself from a dream state, I couldn't tell if I was fully awake. The streetlights from outside were just popping on and the minor league stadium across the way was lit up. The farm team had a double header today. Fireworks would let me know later if they won. That would also mean, fireworks or not, Cooper's would be packed.

Punching the button on my cell left the screen black. The battery was dead. Searching in the dimly lit office I found the end of the charger and plugged it in. I used my time to head down the hall and take a piss. When I got back to the dark office, my phone was lit. It was nearly 8 o'clock and I was thirsty.

Chapter 6

Holding the pistol in my hand felt good, it felt right, and I wanted to use it bad. With no one to point it at, I pointed at myself. Helpless.

Cooper's was busier than I wanted it to be. The long bar was nearly full of mostly young professionals about thirty, having beers and taking shots. They were in their suits and skirts and laughed extra loud. I was forced to take one of the only open seats on the very end of the bar. I sat down. No one ever sat here because the bar wrapped around putting you directly in front of a beer cooler blocking you from the two bartenders on duty. Mumbling as I sat the two women immediately to my right looked over and then went back to talking, moving their hands faster than their mouths as they carried on the conversation. Their voices may have been loud but at least their perfume wasn't.

Leaning to my right I finally made eye contact with the bartender, Alysa the pretty blond from before. She locked eyes with me and instantly began to bounce my way. Her tight body wrapped in a black tank top and little khaki shorts was too much to look away from. Her allure was too hard to avoid but I wished she wasn't here tonight; I wish I wasn't here tonight. I wanted to be alone with a bottle, but desperately needed the distraction of other people, if for nothing more than to simply watch. This bar was a great place for that.

My posture was poor leaving my head low. Alysa lowered her head to meet my eyes, "What can I getcha?" She tossed a cardboard coaster my way. "Oatmeal Stout, right?"

I wanted to agree, and she wanted me to as well. I sighed, "Not tonight." I leaned further to my right, stretching my neck to see the top shelf bourbons and nearly catching the back hand of the broad next to me, "Give me your top shelf bourbon to start."

"Oh, celebrating good news?" Her smile broadened showing more perfect white teeth.

I nodded, "I'm just out remembering the good times."

She was confused by my encrypted words but managed to maintain the smile as she bounced off to pour my drink.

That first gulp went down slow and easy. The flavors of cinnamon, pear and fired oak bounced off my tongue and made me think of my lips as pleasure centers. I took my time and let the bourbon drown out the noise. I couldn't see the televisions mounted on the wall from my cheap seat, so I glanced around at the patrons. The crowd was always a little older here and I liked that. Youth is forever wasted on the young and watching that always makes me sick. The chatter was muffled and indistinguishable to me on the end.

The bourbon warmed my face and allowed the muscles to loosen. I smiled to the heavily eye shadowed lady on my right. She passed for attractive with light brown hair styled big for her night out. Her friend was a copy in a tight skirt and low-cut top. They were in their early thirties. I could tell the one furthest away was in a committed relationship because she never looked beyond her friend. The one next to me talked more, often perusing the bar with a hunter's eye, in the short moments her friend got words in. This one was hungry for something more than the fried bar food. Judging by the tone of the conversation it was as a recent break up. More bourbon and better conversation could get me interested. It would be easy to forget with this one, she was self-centered enough to push any last thought of Pope out of my mind and make me concentrate on her. My battle buddy deserved more; my eyes moved on.

Alysa stepped into view at the other end of the bar, making the universal signal for another round. I nodded and she poured, the beginning of a great relationship. When she served it, I gave her a flushed smile and told her thank you.

"You got it. Where's your friend?" She lingered a moment. Her lower lip curled as she bit it. There were customers who needed drinks, but she stayed to hear what I had to say.

"He's in a better place."

Her face held a questions mark.

I smiled, "Like better as in heading for home and out of Daytona."

Alysa laughed and agreed it was indeed best he get out while he can. She's a true local who remains in the vortex that keeps so many of us here. Then she proceeded to tell me about her night, how they had a rush early and she was in the weeds until help arrived and then it dropped off and now it's steady. It was hard to control my face in a manner that let her think I cared. I didn't, but in that moment as she flicked back her blond hair and rolled her bouncing green eyes, I had forgotten Pope and I was okay with that because I knew he would be too.

As she faded off to the other end of the bar, the crowd overwhelmed me once more. Celebrating alone would be easier alone. It was no one's business why I was celebrating or what for and I wasn't here to celebrate anything anyone else had done. Suddenly I began to hate them, all of them in their afterhours attire. They were all so smart in their *going out* outfits.

I dropped a couple of wrinkled twenties on the bar and left.

A few blocks down and around the corner was a dive called *Baldie's*. I didn't really like to hang out there because a lot of guys I knew hung out there. A normal guy would want to be with friends but when your friends are all crooks, you try to keep your distance. Most nights there was a white van parked across the street and we all knew some agency was sitting in it watching and listening. Tonight, I saw no van, it was going to be a busy night.

Just before I reached the door to Baldie's, I noticed something move. There in the space between buildings' thin alley way, was a slumped over silhouette. A not all too uncommon site outside the bar, I started to move on but again my eyes went to the lumpy mass.

I peered in, stepping a few feet closer and called out, "Hey, you alright?"

I got no response, so I moved a little closer and closer still until the light from the back of the building filled the split between buildings. That's when I recognized my t-shirt and shorts and the guy wearing them.

Pope was lying with his head to side and white creamy vomit with grey specks of burger mixed in it, dripped from his mouth. The whites of his eyes shown between the narrow slits of his lids. I stepped over him and felt his face. It was still warm. I pulled the needle from his arm and untied the band. Then I dragged him out of the alley to the back of the building.

I slid my back down the wall to a seated position and pulled him on my lap. I couldn't feel a pulse but there was the slightest amount of air passing through his nose. I cradled his head and wiped the vomit from his chin. I told him about why I ran out into the darkness that night just before we graduated basic. I told how I was an addict too, that it was nothing to be ashamed of and I was getting help. I was a private eye now and I was going to help people instead of steal from them.

I began rocking ever so slightly as I told him once he was better, I would be a better wing man for him, that he would find a nice girl and settle down. His unconscious mind listened while I planned out the rest of his life, the wife, the kids, and the dog that pees on my tires every time I come to visit.

Pope never woke up. His breathing stopped and eventually there in my arms his body went cold.

From a pay phone, a block away I called 911. Then I went into Baldie's and started drinking.

At some point, after the ambulance left and the police officer took the yellow tape down, I decided to stumble back to my office.

I went in and straight to the lower cabinet drawer. I put the Glock in my pocket and left.

*****

The pool hall was boarded up. I banged on the plywood over the doors begging Delroy or any other dealer to show his face. Eventually I sat on the curb and caught my breath. No one showed.

I drove straight to Kirby's house. Just the blue glow of a television in the living shown through the pale cream curtains. I chugged what was left of my energy drink and headed in.

The cheap brass knob was unlocked and turned easy. I stepped through onto the plastic matt. There in the electric glow of the TV was the old white-headed granny of Kirby. She looked over at me with cobwebbed eyes and sniffed.

"That you, Kirby Baby?"

I walked past her to the back bedroom. He wasn't there, he wasn't in the bathroom or any of the other rooms. Granny caught on quick I wasn't her baby, Kirby.

"Nah, whoever you is, he ain't here, understand?" she said reaching out for a cane that was inches from her finger tips.

"Do you know where he is?"

"He good boy officer, whatever he done he knows it wrong."

"I'm not a cop."

"Lord, no. Then you a white man come to do harm."

I stood with a nine-millimeter pistol pointed at an old grandmother who couldn't see the barrel, believing her grandson wouldn't hurt anyone. I still had the bruises from our encounter a few nights ago. I should have just killed him then. Now I was going to make him hurt as I was hurting.

The Glock was leveled off at her cotton white head. My palm was sweating, and my finger felt slimy on the trigger. My hand, a hand that could dial in a combination lock on a safe was shaking beyond control now. The sweat trickled down from the grip, down off my wrist.

"Kirby, he gets me my medicine." She reached a shaky hand out for the TV tray to her left. She knocked over a brown pill bottle and some weed rolled out. She felt for it and put some into a pipe. She smoked the pipe and with smoke coming from her mouth said, "It's for my glaucoma."

I sat on the plastic covered sofa to her right. The old black and white movie ended, and Perry Como came on to sing Some Enchanted Evening as the credits shown.

A smile came across the old woman's mouth, and I saw the silver of her bridge. "Nah that Perry can sing a good tune. He ain't my Nate Cole, but he alright."

She somehow found me in her blindness. The two grey eyes peered at me through the darkness of the living room. "Everyone is capable of good." She said, "I knows this, I know my Kirby do wrong but he do good to me and his sisters. He gets them up for school and makes sure they get home. He a good boy mister. Nah I ask you, what good gonna come of you killin' my Kirby?"

I left her sitting there.

"Hello? You still there mister?"

The crowd was still thirsty at Cooper's. It all looked so joyous I wanted to blow salt in their eyes. Alysa was the only thing standing in the way of soaking their livers in alcohol. She bounced about, pouring, and refilling drinks.

She slung me something I didn't order, but I drank it back fast. My stomach tightened and flopped; I was going to vomit. I started to regain my composure as the rationalizations flooded into my mind. Denial was emboldened by an unwillingness to seek the truth myself. My palms were beginning to sweat as two voices shouted each other down in my head. The voices wouldn't stop telling me what I did right and what I did wrong.

I shouted the voices down, but they came back strong, this time with images of Pope. He was smiling then, dead in my arms.

The voices in my head faded, the whiskey was working, but soon new voices penetrated my mind. These were the voices of the fellow patrons. They were near and far, loud, and soft. The one laughing was the worse. Then the women next to me started and never stopped. I gritted my teeth and curled my fist.

Alysa read the distress on my face, "Hey I gotcha' down here!" She shouted over the crowd and pointed to an empty booth near the other end of the bar, closer to the serving station.

I nodded and moved. She dropped the tall glass down and I swooped it up. I cocked my head to an empty booth, and she nodded. She was a mind reader and a life saver. I needed to be alone but close enough to allow for the possibility of interacting. What a strange dichotomy I entered. To laugh and talk would be to forget Pope and I wasn't ready for that. So, I sat with my drink and watched everyone else do that for me.

The server came to the table a few more times, she took the empties and replaced them with a full glass. Every time food was offered, I passed. My stomach still churned thinking about Pope. I was tired of their laughter; their good time was pissing me off. It was time to leave. There was eighty in stolen drug dealer cash on the table, I hoped it was enough. I scooted to the edge of the seat, as I stood there was a smiling face inches from my own.

"Hey there neighbor." Chloe said with a laugh. Her hair held curls and she had on lots of makeup. A rush of musk finishing in sweet honey flavored my tongue as I breathed her in. She was flanked by two equally done-up girls, both looking annoyed at having to stop by my corner of the bar.

I smiled a drunken smile. Chloe's eyes danced over the table, "You leaving already? I just got here." Her smile was straight and sober. Her scent and make-up still fresh, she had not been drenched in a night of excess. She had a foreign body with a familiar face, a perfect complement to the now quieted voices in my head. So, when she asked if I would like to join them at the other end of the bar, I nodded yes, and the voices detested me for accepting.

We bumped and bounced off people making our way to the only two open seats. I stood and let Chloe sit along with one of her friends. The two friends luckily did not last long as they spotted some other girls they knew and quickly moved back to where we just left. Apparently, I ruined girls' night, it was my *not interested* funk, the stink I showed and repelled all who got close.

"You can head down there with them if you want, I'm not much for socializing tonight." I sipped my whiskey expecting her to leave.

"And miss out seeing you drunk? No, I'll stay right here." She laid four long fingers on my thigh and squeezed with her manicured thumb.

There was an electric charge in my body. It had been so long that being touched like that, my reaction was to withdraw but the alcohol numbed me well and I leaned in. With the sounds of the dead quiet in my mind I could hear Chloe's words but never what she was saying. I smiled and laughed and nodded a lot. She kept on and so did the booze.

The hands on the clock passed like our hands on each other. With each pass, they lingered longer and longer. My eyes drifted away from her face and like a topographer I studied every peak and valley on the map of her body. Her dress was painted on and with her body it could be. She knew where my eyes were going, how they raked over her skin, and clawed at her dress wanting to rip it off.

The bar tender broke our gaze asking us for another round. Chloe whispered in my ear, "You got booze at your place?" I nodded and we cashed out.

The walk to the office was a stumbling haze. The air was dense and clung to my skin. In the distance a rumble came as the black sky went bright, exposing impenetrable, charged, clouds throwing electricity at each other. Soon those clouds would break, and the release would wash away the grime building on our bodies. By the time we reached my floor, my shirt was off, and her lipstick was smeared on my face, neck, and chest. She stopped there in the hall and cupped my shoulders. A painted nail traced over my clavicles and up and down my neck then back to my shoulders and down my tattooed biceps.

She made a little growl and said, "You're just such a man, Grimes." I smirked at the obvious, but she continued, "No I mean I've seen muscular guys at the gym, but you, you're so wide and I know in those endless blue eyes, it's like you're a caveman and you've dragged me back to your cave. You're the last of the knuckle draggers, Roger Grimes." With a shudder she melted like butter in my hot hands as I held her to me, her body melding into mine.

My office became a cave and my couch a bed of animal hides. We began to rip each other apart until we had turned each other inside out. The barking night sky broke and dumped lifesaving water down on the city, washing away the filth that had clung to every sidewalk and alleyway. The thunder rolled through the building rattling the windows as she straddled my lap. I sat erect and ran my hand up the back of her neck eventually palming the base of her skull. Her hair intertwined in my fingers, and I had complete control. She leaned back as my lips covered her neck down to her perfect teardrop breasts. My hands cupped each one as I tightened my grip to feel them in my hands. The lightning flashed and, in that instant, I could see in her eyes she was ready.

Hours in the gym had perfectly molded Chloe's body to shapes that any man should be enthralled with. I let her curves work me into an idol worship trance. In the temple of her figure, I moved with deliberate force. Her sounds guttural as sweat began to flush our systems of the toxic alcohol we consumed to bring us here.

I turned her around. Her knees buried into the cushions on the couch as her hands gripped the back of it. I took a handful of that blond hair with one hand and held her hip with my other. We joined together gently at first then slipped into an ever-aggressive rhythm until the slapping of our colliding bodies were shouted down by her cries of ecstasy.

My mind escaped our gripped bodies and ascended so that I was looking down at what we were doing. Her sculped body at its physical peak, hours of spin class and squats, was not enough to keep me. Images of Ronald emerging from the glory hole in the pool hall bathroom returned. The girl that ran out of the back, had it been a young girl? A runaway?

There, connected as one, she could sense what I was feeling and that she was losing me. Attaching a years' worth of flirting was not enough. She wasn't going to let that happen and took control. Spinning us around, directing me with the core of her body until we were interlocked once more, this time she was in control. The caveman laid down his club. I leaned back, watching her respond to my subtle movements until finally our eyes locked once more and liberation was all we needed.

Chloe collapsed onto my chest, heaving for every breath, she said, "Why'd you make me wait all this time Grimes?" She pushed off me with a grin from ear to ear as sweat beaded across her brow.

With a smile on my own face I said, "Good things come to those who wait." I slapped her thigh and got up for a bottle of water from the mini fridge. She sat naked on the couch with her legs crossed, not to reject but as to not distract from her analysis of me as I stood, just a black silhouette against the black windowpane. Halfway through with the bottle I came up for air and crossed the office floor to hand her the bottle. She drank from it without taking her eyes from my frame.

I had sunk in next to her on the couch. She turned her back into my shoulder and brought her knees up to her chest. Her yellow hair was in my face leaving strands clinging to my stubble.

"Looks like you're doing well for yourself here Grimes." She said looking around at my office.

A/C kicked sending a cool subtle breeze to pass over us. I reached behind and grabbed an old woven Mexican blanket and draped it over our bodies. "I work for a lawyer named Willis Sanford now."

She hummed and nodded adding she had seen his billboard. We went on to make chit chat about things we didn't cover over drinks. It would have been nice and normal for her to stay there with me on the couch and keep my thoughts of failing Pope at bay, but eventually the thoughts returned, and I could no longer hear what she was saying.

Chloe got up and rolled that tight black dress over her shoulders and shimmied it down the rest of her rises and curves. Her mouth moved expelling excuses as to why she couldn't stay. The reasons weren't important to me. I now wanted her gone as much as she wanted to leave. She went on to say she was worried about Tab being exposed to things, to the crap out in the world. Things are different when you have kids, she left me with that advice or warning, I don't know. Either way that comment lingered in my mind longer than my need to see her again.

After she left, I sat by the light of my tablet on my face, wrapped in the blanket with my feet up on my desk. There was something circling my brain like a shark smelling blood but could not find the meal. I knew it was out there in the afloat in the deep dark ocean of the mind. Something she said, it was about Tab and how being a parent changed her forever. The mother holding her child during a bank robbery, the teenage prostitute at a drug dealer's apartment, and whoever was in the pool hall bathroom. My heart sank into my whiskey filled belly. Shit.

I tapped out a reply to Gregg Hines's email.

> ***Sorry for this late reply. I have no immediate leads, but I am willing to help in any way possible. I will call you tomorrow and we can go over the details.***

Once it was sent, my eyes began to burn with a beckon to be closed. I crawled under the blanket and watched out the widow as angry clouds fought, throwing white lightning somewhere off the coast over the Atlantic.

Chapter 7

Getting back to work was all I had. It's the only way out of this.

I poured the last of the grounds in the coffee maker and hit the switch. A clean shirt was lifted from the closet, and I went down the hall to the common bathroom. Inside I splashed cold water to my face, ran wet fingers over my buzzed scalp and then used the old t-shirt to scrub my arm pits. After my morning constitution, I opened the door to a line of men in shirts with ties and shiny shoes. The glam life of living in the office had worn off and I was ready to move up a floor with a private bathroom.

Finally, close to two in the afternoon I sat with a coffee cup steaming with savory black coffee and took a seat on the couch with the tablet. My fiasco with Pope and his death left me gun shy about what I was doing. Everything I had worked for was suddenly worthless to me. My friend was drowning and me the hero, threw him a cement life preserver. Now he was dead, and my only friend left was pissed at me. There was still forty-seven fifty that I stole in the bag. It was bad form to start spending it now and I still wanted to somehow get my share back to Billy. I checked my bank account and stared at the balance then snagged a few twenties from the stack and shoved them in my wallet. I closed that website out and went to my email. Besides the usual spam there was one reply in there. It was from someone who needed my help.

Men who can crack a safe while knowing full well an armed security guard will be making his rounds shortly, usually do not get sweaty palms. At this moment, reading over the email of a new prospective client, my palms went wet. Before reading further, several thoughts crossed my mind, there were things to do, forms to have filled out and money to collect. Are taxes charged? I would have to Google that latter. Right now, I needed more on the case.

I dialed. The voice on the other line was boisterous and spilling over with confidence. A little hesitation on my part as I asked again if I was speaking with Gregg Hines. Hines assured me and asked what he could do for me.

"Well, you emailed me about Milo." I had a pen and a note pad out. The ballpoint scrapped along the paper doing circles to ensure ink flow.

"I surely did. Say can you hang on a quick sec?" Gregg let his words hang. There was a little shuffling on his end and then with the breeze raking over the mic he said, "Sorry about that. I had to get out of my office." This time it was the voice of a worried father who had not slept in several nights.

"Yeah. So can you come down to my office?"

"Oh, okay. That would be best wouldn't it. I never used a private investigator before, I wasn't, you know, sure. I didn't even think you read my email." A nervous chuckle lead to more raking of the breeze over his mic.

"I'll text you the address. What time do you think you can make it?"

There was a pause, just the wind again coming through, "I, I have to," He was silent, I could hear the noises of the street in his silence then he said, "you know what I'll be there as soon as I can."

"I'm always here." I hung up. I hated talking on the phone when I knew I would see him here tonight face to face. I texted out the address and got an immediate reply. There it was the next paying client.

An easy internet search produced the information I was looking for. Gregg Hines was a lobbyist to the state. His backers were anti-death penalty and anti-gun. His criminal record was nonexistent, and his known associates all appeared to be politicians and corporate leaders, which to me was the same as crooks. Yale educated with the only blemish on his record was a failed run for state representative.

All in all, he was a standup guy on paper. With a semi-public life I could see why he did not want to go to the cops on this one. His friends included some very prominent citizens, current senators, a former president and many more Florida elected public servants. For once the idea of being severely under qualified resonated through my body.

Chapter 8

Everyone wants to put you in a box they can check off. If you wear two hats you are praised as a hard worker, if you have two faces you are the most vial scum. I have been doing both and burning the candle at four ends.

It took Gregg twenty-eight minutes to get to my office. He knocked softly. I could hear the man on the other side of the door clear his throat.

The father was taller than I expected and older too. He stood a lanky six foot six. His black, short sleeve button down shirt exposed purple and blue veins in both his arms, mostly around the wrists. His blue jeans were crisp and clean. Large hands wiped perspiration off and then the right one went out. I grabbed it. Gregg's shake was firm and quick.

The father sat on the couch. His face was long with a silvery five o'clock shadow sprouting out. The rest of his hair was a mix of salt and pepper that looked overdue for a trim. He had that look of sleepless nights and frayed nerves. His pain projected from every pore and radiated out over the office. The guilt for not taking his call sooner coagulated on my shoulders curving my back and forcing my head closer to the desk.

The silence was vast. I needed to fill it but could not find the words. My inexperience oozed as I shifted in my seat.

"Willis seems to think you above any other can find my Milo." Gregg rubbed his palms together. He was more professional than I.

I sat up. "I hope so." I took out a pen and scribbled it on a note pad. "Tell me everything."

Gregg leaned his long torso over the edge of the couch and began to recount his daughter's life as he knew it, where she was born, how she looked and what her grades had been through school, right up until she ran off. His face aged, the lines grew deep across his forehead as he mumbled the statistics of late. His fingers scraped the corners of his mouth. Before he continued, I offered him something to drink.

Gregg opted for the beer, my last PBR. Half of the golden lager was gone before he came up for air. Now he was able to tell me what I really needed to know.

"Milo is mad at me. After her mother passed things got off balanced. She's gotten mixed up with this boy, or young man. I don't, maybe seventeen or eighteen years of age. His name is Jinky. Doubtful that is his real name." Gregg finished the beer. With wide eyes he looked around my office as if just arriving. Giving me this bit of information seemed all too revealing for him.

"What do the cops have on Jinky?" If it was a street name, there wasn't much street in it.

"I never reported it." His large hand spread across his face. "I thought this was something I could handle on my own, but now I, I am so afraid of what happened to her."

My foot began to tap as my knee bounced to jazz music I couldn't hear. He was withholding information from the cops. Milo was a young girl missing and he was holding back. I wanted to jump up and smack him.

"This might have been over if you shared that info with the cops. Mr. Hines, I don't think you need me on this. I don't know what Sanford told you when he recommended me but, I just..." I let my self-dismissal hang there waiting for him to cap with his assurance of giving it another try with the police.

"Roger, I screwed up, but I stand by that mistake. I just couldn't, I couldn't let the police know those details of what Milo was in to. It just," He shut his eyes, pinching them tight. A thin clear string of snot began to run from his nose. His face was beat red when he opened his eyes once more.

"I have been searching for her."

His eyes brightened just a bit as some of the red faded to pink.

Before his hopes rose too high, I said, "It would help if I knew more about her. Where she likes to hang out, any friends besides Jinky."

"I'm afraid I wasn't around much, I never got to know any of her friends. With my job, I travel to Washington often."

"And it's because of your job, you want this kept quiet."

He nodded. "The boy's around town somewhere."

I nodded. "Why not find him and go get her?"

Gregg stood, wiped his watery eyes and then wiped his hands on his pant legs, "I'm not you Grimes." He extended a large open hand. I stood to shake it. He left without any more words.

I stood bewildered. This old man was in pain enough just imagining where is daughter is, I didn't want to draw him a picture. This town attracted runaways and there was always one sure way to make money as a runaway. The possibilities were eating Hines up inside and for good reason. Pride in a public career was more important than his daughter's wellbeing. Milo deserved better than Gregg Hines for a father.

Perhaps if I had more experience or if I had that knack to keep people talking, ask all the right questions, I could have got him to stay. This whole thing could be easily resolved, and I might have more money in my account to use towards a rack of ribs. My stomach complained out loud, and I am not a talker. My stomach and I both would have to settle on the mostly frozen burrito from the mini fridge.

Before the timer hit zero, my phone rang. It was a blocked number and I almost let it go but with this new P.I. job I would have to learn new habits.

"Yeah,"

"I need you to see this through to the end. All the way to the end."

I recognized the voice. Sanford was using a burner. I let him talk without asking questions, something my P.I. courses didn't teach but life as a criminal did.

"Did Hines give you enough to go on?"

"I think so," I said. "I got something I want you to look over. Might be of some use."

"Okay, send it. And remember, see this through to the end."

"I got it."

The line went dead. My burrito was done but I just wanted a drink.

Cooper's was dead. It was just before five in the evening and the sun had just made it over to the other side of the buildings casting long shadows out over the street, reaching to the sea wall on the brown river. I took my seat at the empty bar and stared up at the TV's. Whoever the bartender was, they weren't around to take orders.

I sat and typed out a text to Sanford, attaching the pictures from Delroy' computer of the spreadsheets. Sanford was a man of means, success and well known. If there was anything worthwhile buried on those sheets, he'd find it.

Ready to pour myself a stout, Alysa came out from the kitchen behind me. Her normally perfectly pulled back blonde hair was filled with fly-aways. Her tight green shirt had a couple stains to cap her rough day.

"Hey," she smiled, "what can I getcha?" She tucked a stained bar towel in her belt.

"I'll take a Breakfast Blend."

She sucked her teeth through a frowning grin. "Just ran out. You'll have to wait until I can get someone to change the keg."

"Okay," I looked over the taps, nothing was enticing my taste buds. "I'll take a water."

Alysa turned her back to get the water and said over her shoulder, "Staying off the hard stuff tonight?"

There was nobody in the bar, but a crash from the kitchen reminded me we were not totally alone. Sanford's cryptic call had my stomach acid in revolt. The acid churned as my mind free cycled with no resistance. I didn't know where to find a young punk named Jinky.

I went through the first two waters without ordering anything else. Two women came in, looked around and left.

"Slow night?" I asked Alysa who was leaning against the inside of the bar looking up at the TV with the remote in her hand. The guide was up, and she was scrolling through shows that normally don't belong in a bar, History Channel and HGTV.

She looked over her shoulder, "Ah, I can use the break." She turned around, saw I was down to the ice and grabbed my glass. "Ball game last night and the manger didn't staff for it. He's cutting hours to make sure he hits his bonus."

"Dick move."

"Yep." She set the ice water down on the soggy coaster. "Third water? That lady you went home with must have really worn you out."

Before I could reply some teenagers came in. There were four of them, two girls and two guys. They were in a tight ball and giggled with goofy grins. Alysa walked down to the end of the bar where they stood. She told them they could sit anywhere, meaning the tables but they all sat at the bar.

"I'll need to see some I.D. if you're planning on sitting at the bar." Alysa said resting her hands on the bar.

The blond guy from the group pulled his I.D. out quickly from a front pocket. Rookie mistake when passing a fake. Alysa barely had to look it over before handing it back.

"Nice try. Maybe it works over on the beachside at one of those clubs but not here." She stood back and crossed her arms. The other three lost their will to pull one over on Alysa and they all slinked out with their heads hung.

Alysa turned back, "Like I've never seen a fake before?"

I dropped some bills on the bar and walked out.

****

The V-8 under the hood rumbled as I circled the blocks consisting of the club scene in town. There was only a handful of places for teenagers to hang out. Hitting clubs that were known for letting in the underage, allowed them to mix with adults.

I pulled around the club for a third time. There was no choice but to park and walk. I drove up and turned right. It was a busy night on the beachside. Young ones were out, spring break maybe, but too late in the year for that. I had to think about what time of year it is, with barely two seasons, losing track of the year is easy.

I drove along, crawling, waiting for a spot to open then I saw a familiar face. The face was lit by his cell phone, identifying him as he walked along the sidewalk.

I leaned out the window, "James."

James stopped cold. His head popped up like a prairie dog and looked side to side. After he spotted me, he bolted.

I threw the truck in reverse and smoked the tires.

He was trapped with buildings to his right and me to his left. He couldn't outrun me, so he stopped and cut left. I hit the brakes and punched it forward, again laying rubber.

I watched him jump a low chain keeping people out of an empty bank parking lot and run for a fence. I swung around the corner and caught him making it across the street. I sped forward to the light and got lucky with a long yellow. We both cut left and went west down Sea Breeze Avenue.

James ran along and began to lose steam as he neared the corner. I was caught behind a car at the light. Breathing heavy, he held on to the light pole and looked both ways trying to decide which way to run. He looked up and saw the light was changing. In a panic he cut across Halifax and headed down towards the river.

I leapt the truck over the intersection and down under the bridge that crossed the Intercostal Waterway. The engine roared as the exhaust echoed off the concrete bridge above. Under the bridge the lights of the city were blacked out. The water sloshed against the coral rocks, leaving a tan colored foam behind. I caught a whiff of salty air. If getting away from me was his objective, James chose the worse place.

At the end of the little peninsula, jetting out into the river, James crouched behind some coquina rocks. I parked the truck and slowly walked over. To his left were a couple of bums, blacked out from the days drink.

I stood at the edge of the asphalt, "James, I'm not a cop and I'm not going to hurt you."

James's bright white eyes stood out from the blackness that surrounded him. His fingers moved along the top of the coquina. He righted himself and moved slowly out.

"You ain't no cop, then what you want?" he said moving into the soft yellow glow of the nightlife behind us.

"I'm looking for someone and I thought maybe you could help."

"Who the fuck are you? I don't know you."

I remembered I was wearing a mask the night I jumped him and took his money. I felt so stupid I chuckled to myself which only increased his paranoia.

"No, you don't." I said pushing the ruse. "I was told you were a man who knew people. I need to know someone." I reached in my pocket. His body tensed. My hand came out with some green. He watched me peel back a couple Jacksons and I handed them out.

James approached like a stray dog cautious of the hand feeding him. After he shoved them in his pocket he said, "How you get my name?"

"James, if I told you that then I would never be told anything again. No names, I don't use one and the person I'm after won't know yours, see how this works?"

James nodded sharply. He was swaying a little and looking side to side. His breathing was still labored. "So, what you want?"

"I'm looking for a guy named, Jinky."

James looked around some more. I noticed the lump above his eye I put there a few nights ago and the palms of his hands were still skinned from when he fell.

"Yeah, he's a pervy little guy. No offense if you're related." James dropped the street talk for more of a regular college kid dialect.

I peeled off a couple more Jacksons, for pain and suffering from the other night.

"So do you know where I can find him?"

His eyes rolled up to the corner of their sockets, he was thinking hard, digging for a true answer.

"I don't hang out with him. Find him on Facebook or something, he posts a lot."

"You got a real name for him?"

James thought some more, "It's the same as some actor."

"Oh, right that one, c'mon."

"I know if you saw his face, damn." He went to his phone and started searching. After a minute of us standing in the dark under the bridge James looked up with a smile.

"Matthew Perry." he said proudly.

"Thanks Jimmy." I handed over the twenties. James shoved them quickly into his pocket.

"Yeah, I know you from some place."

"You get yourself a new job yet, something more legal than dealing drugs?" I grinned and started back for my truck.

I heard him whisper *Shit* under his breath. Yeah, he knew me.

Chapter 9

The sun will still rise tomorrow no matter what is done in the dark. From light to dark to light again, that is the way it goes.

Social media told me Jinky would be at the skating rink. Nearing the rink, my left leg tremored into a bounce as a pit opened in my gut. Sanford's cryptic words to see it through circled my brain. I knew what he meant, what he wanted me to do. My mind tried to bend it, work around it and be altruistic with thoughts of arrests and reunions. Deputy Camp told me that was not the way this world worked. Sanford knew I had profited from the dark side of the real world for a long time. Pay a little extra won't get you a happy ending here, we are just constantly moving until one day we stop, and I was no exception.

Sitting in my truck outside the skating rink, I studied the kid's social media. It's so easy to get all the dope on someone these days when they post every minute of their lives online. Jinky had so many selfies from every direction I had a 3D composite. He looked to be thin with long hair on top of his head and shaved around the sides. In many of the photos he was wearing black eyeliner and his clothes always seemed to hug tight to his slender frame. Intimidating this punk would be easy. I could be back at the bar in under an hour with Milo safe in her room getting ready for bed.

The skating rink was packed. Either it was the weekend or summertime already. In this state summer starts around April and runs through October. It's easy to lose track of the months when there are only two seasons. I got out of the truck and left my piece in the glove box on purpose, ignoring conscious reasoning.

I went through the doors and joined the line at the ticket window. A pretty, slender blond with sparkly eyes of youth was framed by a black wooden booth that opened to an adjacent counter inside the rink. She flung her long hair over her shoulder as she talked to the people in line before me. She sported qualities that made me think this was how Chloe must have looked twenty years ago. As those thoughts scrolled across my mind, I could feel my eyes grow large. Chloe, here I was thinking about her in the middle of a case, while tracking down a dirt bag twenty-something with a taste for the young ones. The knot in my gut flipped. I knew what that meant. Now was not the time to get gooey over some hot-mom, I needed her out of my system.

"Hi," she said with a smile that bounced off the glass.

"Yeah, ah my kid was dropped off earlier. I'll just need one ticket." I had no idea what I was asking for. I didn't know if they sold tickets or stamped your hand or what. She waited for me to produce the cash and I slid it under the window. She slid back the change and a ticket. I heard the electric lock buzz on the door and pushed through.

The skating rink was the same as every skating rink. Flashing lights and blaring music with the circular rink in the middle. This was just the PG version of the R rated club. Way to train them up, I thought, but we all did it and I turned out, well, not so good.

Straight ahead was the rink. To the left of the skates, video arcade and concession. Jinky didn't strike me as too athletic so I doubted he would be out on the rink. I skipped the skates and grabbed a coke at the concession and a seat at one of the long picnic style tables.

I went through a few cokes and a few trips to the bathroom without catching a look at anyone who even resembled Jinky. My first job as a P.I. I caught a lucky break and got the evidence I needed fast. It felt great at the time and now more like a set up. My success came too early.

My rounded off belly couldn't take another coke, so I decided it was time to leave. Outside, night had won the battle with day. Low cloud cover kept the ambient light in, giving the night sky a purplish grey hue. The asphalt was damp from a light shower that had blown through leaving the air thick and clinging to my skin. I saw some middle school aged kids gathered around the corner of the skate rink. Excited faces on bouncing heads spread out to form a semi-circle. Large, engaged eyes dispersed electricity, static charging the air. It was a familiar scene, something that happens all too often at that age, a fight was coming.

Even at my age, the level-headed adult, I felt that rumble in my gut as I approached the hungry pack of adolescents looking to climb the wild jungle's pecking order. I joined in the free-floating angst carried on charged particles as I neared the shouting match between two young teen girls. Their back packs were long ago stripped as the dance had already begun, side stepping each other in a circular motion as the lookers-on shouted, a few held-up cell phones to make sure it went out to all the social media world.

Each girl with a snarl and pinched eyes waiting for the other to act, the crowd wanted blood, and these two gladiators had no choice now. One girl, fair skinned and freckled pulled her black curly hair back and quickly wrapped a rubber band around the bun. The other girl, a brown skin mixed girl had her hands up flickering motion with her fingers to invite the white girl to strike. The verbal assault had already commenced, and the crowd was eating it up with "Ooohh", and more hopping around as each word landed a blow.

"Hey!" I barked and in a knee jerk reaction to always being in trouble half the crowd ran off. A few brave or loyal ones lingered. I marched in quickly, not completely sure what I was going to say. It didn't matter because I spotted what I really wanted, one of the kids with a cell phone held high live streaming the fight was Jinky. I kept him in my peripheral vision as I told the kids to break it up. He did his best to melt away.

The adult man did not have to try hard to mix with the young teens. He was skinny and lanky with few black hairs on his pasty white chin. His black hair was greasy and parted on the side. Despite the warm night, he wore a yellow windbreaker and black skinny jeans.

The two girls mouthed off to each other as they slowly fell apart, freed from the ever-tightening circle of excited youth. I watched Jinky with my full attention now as he kept his back to me and wandered off towards the neighboring parking lot. I slowed my pace, keeping him at my two o'clock. He glanced back, then quickened his steps. Once the crowd disappeared, I silently jogged towards Jinky.

I caught hold of his shoulder just as his paranoid instincts told him to check for me one more time. His eyes grew and his upper lip curled. He showed me his palms as he put up his hands, dropping his cell phone.

"Easy," I said trying to keep him from pissing his skinny jeans. "I need to talk to you."

"Whoa, you scared the shit outta me." He looked down at his phone and scooped it up saying, "Shit, shit, please don't be cracked." Then as he cradled his precious, he let out a little gleeful giggle. I felt like fileting off my skin and spraying myself down with a firehose hooked to a hydrant of bleach to get his creepiness out of my mind.

"Hope it's not broken." I said calmly.

"No, all good." Jinky came down from his scare and looked around as if the lights suddenly flipped on. It was just us out in a dark parking lot a hundred yards from anyone. Fear glazed his expression and held his tongue.

"I need to find a girl. There's easy money in it for you if you help."

"I don't know, go to a club. There's plenty of drunk chicks looking to hook up." He went back to the blue glow of his cell, connecting with the online world. I stood silently. He looked up from his phone. "What man? I can't help you."

"I'm not a cop. I just, I heard you were the guy to see about finding a date." I put my hands in my pockets and hung my head to shrink my large frame.

Jinky looked around, at the distance to the rink and the road beyond that. A single car passed under the lights of the road. He flipped through his phone swiping and tapping.

"Pimps." He chirped and grinned. "There's pimps for that."

"A friend, Randel Brume said you were the guy. I got cash."

"Randy huh? You know Randy?"

I nodded.

"What's he look like?" Jinky flipped up his chin at me with a challenge.

"Kinda dorky, glasses, balding," I said.

"Yeah, that's him. Okay, I can help you." The fear was rolled back, and he stood a little taller, swallowed and continued, "I don't normally connect you directly, you see there are, um, I don't want to be rude but people who handle that."

I looked blankly, inside I left myself unsure what he was getting at, not wanting him to go there.

My stomach wretched but I kept my cool. "Ah, I sure would appreciate your help." I hung my head as I whispered. I shrunk myself, letting him take the lead.

"Sure doll. Follow me." He turned and started walking and texting. I couldn't get a look at the name he was messaging but they went back and forth the entire time we walked finally stopping at a lime green Scion, the one that looks like toaster. He opened the driver's side door and stood looking down at his phone.

"What's your number? I'll have Stef-fon text you the details." He said without looking up.

I did my best to look sly, "Oh no I can't do that." And shook my head *no*.

Jinky shrugged. "Okay we can go around that. I'll tell him your phone got shut off." He smiled without looking up from his phone. His skinny fingers punched away at the screen. The phone beeped. He giggled, that text was from someone else. Then another text came while he was replying to what made him giggle. Then he opened the text from the pimp.

Jinky looked up, "You clean?"

I shrugged not understanding what he was getting at.

"You know, needle user? Got the hep, herp or hiv? Clean man, you clean?" Jinky held his phone ready to reply to the pimp.

My head nodded, to all his questions. *These poor girls.* Sanford wanting me to take this to the end was becoming easier on my conscious.

Jinky texted and another came back. It was an address that he linked to his map app on the phone. The robotic voice told us how to start our journey.

"They change places every couple of weeks. This is the address if you want to type it in yourself." He showed me the phone.

"Can you take me there?"

Jinky started with excuses, then looked down at the wad of crumpled green bills I held. "Sure thing boss, I'll be your Uber tonight." He giggled and spun on his heels to get in the car.

We got in the car and started out of the parking lot. The rain had rolled through but the wind driving it remained. Few people were on the road as we headed south then west through the shiny wet streets. Jinky was driving me to a place to pick out a young kid and do as I please. He didn't bat an eye when the cash was out, it was all so easy for him. Human beings were nothing but a commodity to him, something stolen and fenced. I knew the process, I knew what it took to disengage, separate the person from their possession. You first rationalize it, convince yourself it didn't mean anything to them. Then just block them out, pretend the owner doesn't exist.

One girl still existed outside of Jinky's mind. Milo had a father who wanted her back, and he had a friend and that friend hired me. We made the branches and Milo was the trunk of this tree of life. She wasn't alone, she had not been forgotten. Her branches may have been trimmed back, and her leaves gone but there was a new spring coming. A chance for a new life.

The small apartment complex was flanked on either side by trailer parks, so it was the Ritz. The three two story buildings formed a horseshoe with parking all in the middle. Each building was painted a dull grey with white trim. The sounds of people going about their lives emanated as pots crashed and babies cried out for attention. A dog barked and the owner yelled.

We pulled into a spot and walked across the parking lot to building C on the right of where we came in. I wouldn't even have noticed the black late model Impala on chrome 22's if it wasn't for the low thump of bass buzzing from the trunk.

As we walked past the Impala the headlights came on, halting us there on the sidewalk in front of Building C. The driver's door opened, and white smoke escaped then a large dark-skinned hand grabbed the roof as the driver pulled himself out. Using a cane in the left hand for support, he stood.

"Yo Jinky," He waved us over. The man was large, heavy and had small dreads in his black hair. I recognized him, I hoped he was not as good with faces.

"What up Luther." Jinky's voice got a little deeper and he walked a little heavier on his heels than when I first met him. His hand went out and so did Luther's.

When their hands slid apart Luther said, "I ain't know you party like dis, wit these hoes."

"Nah, just walking a *virgin* in."

Luther's eyes took a rounder shape now as the smile withdrew. His yellow teeth were still showing as his nose whistled through labored breaths. The door man for the child brothel sized me up. Raking me over with his eyes he searched for a memory. I slouched and kept my head low, anything to alter my form and block his memory from detecting me.

"Kris know you comm'in?" Luther asked Jinky all the while staring at me.

"Yeah, yeah I text him." Jinky forced a smile. Sweat rolled down his temple, slowly gathering, and bonding together to create larger beads that rolled down under their own weight and collect under his jaw.

"A'ight." The big man turned and sat back down into his blacked-out guard's booth on 22's. The bass thumped a little louder as we walked away.

As we hit the stairs I hiked a thumb over my shoulder, "We gonna see any more security like that one?"

Jinky giggled, "Nah, Luther's a fuck up. Didn't you notice his cane? He got shot the other night."

I stopped there in the middle of our ascent for an over dramatic pause, "Over what?"

Jinky was two steps up. He looked back at me, "I guess you wouldn't know unless you dope."

I shook my head "no".

"Yeah, some guy put a huge dent in the heroin trade in town. He jacked up a few dealers and shot up a 3rd Street hangout. No one's been able to buy smack around here since. I guess 3rd street or whoever was supplying them is taking a breather." Jinky turned and bounced up the rest of the steps.

I had convinced myself that Pope's death meant what I did that night was for nothing, especially him. But I see now that it did make a difference. I broke up the flow of H in this town, even if it was just temporary. A few less people got high this week and maybe just one of them stayed sober enough to want help, to crush the habit that has been crushing them. I held on to that positive, mulling it over, forcing it to fill the negative space inside me, and cover the wrong I had done. It wasn't enough, I had more to do now, more positives to get to fill the negatives I've had for so long. Milo would be my next.

On the second floor, halfway down the hall, Jinky stopped and knocked on the door.

"Yeah," came a deep voice on the other side of the door.

"It's me. I got a friend."

The bolt on the door slid back first followed by two chain locks. A waft of damp moldy air clung to my lungs. It was the kind of smell you get from not never changing you're A/C filter and the condensation at the air handler was building up in the unit, soaking into the carpet.

Inside was not any better. The only furniture were two wooden dining room chairs, a small round table with an overflowing ashtray and a TV on a milk crate. In the kitchen there were liquor bottles and red plastic cups. On the stained tile floor were two full plastic trash bags with paper plates and paper towels spilling out. It was a regular squatter's paradise.

The guy who opened the door was slobbering on a blunt. His hair was in a nice fade and wavy at the top and he kept running a flat palm over it as he led us into the apartment. His skin was light and his features round. He had on a white wife beater, long black basketball shorts and white socks with Nike sandals over them.

A sparse mustache on his upper lip wiggled as he said, "Whatch you doin' here Jinky?"

"Just walking up a guy. He's here for a girl."

"No shit." The pimp looked me over. I got the impression he didn't like me.

"I thought T-bag was here tonight."

"Nah, he got a call." The unidentified man looked to me and continued, "So whatch you want playa?"

"Um," I put my hands in my pockets, "I was hoping to find a specific girl, Milo."

The wet blunt went to the corner of the man's mouth as he grinned. His eyes shifted to Jinky who painfully grinned back. Just then a timer in the kitchen went off. Jinky jumped, then let out a now familiar giggle. "Lord, that scared me."

The man laughed, "No Milo here tonight. You got door one and door two" He went to the hall. He leaned with his arm up against the wall, slapping the wall with an open palm he shouted, "Hey yo, times up."

A muffled voice from behind a closed door said, "Five minutes."

"Aw hell no. Now man, I've got customers waiting." He banged on the wall, this time with a fist. He moved down the hall and pushed open a door with splintered indents from a fist. From in the room he yelled, "Joss where the hell you at girl?"

He came out with his shoulders bowed and tight clenched fists. He strode to the only other door in the hall and banged again. "Get out here!"

From inside the bathroom a toilet flushed, and the door came open. Standing, looking up at the pimp was another familiar face. It was the girl from T-bag's place. Her eyes were cat like slits and her claws were out. "Can't I take a shit without you up my ass?"

The man chuckled then grabbed her by the back of the neck, she resisted but was too weak. "Get back to your room. Dumb bitch."

He turned to me, "You can go with her or wait for that one," and pointed to the other door. "Up to you man."

He brushed past me and took a seat on the wooden chair.

Joss paused before going back to her room. Her eyes met mine and darted away quickly.

I looked at Jinky. "Wait for me."

Jinky hesitated then nodded adding, "I'll be in the car."

I went into the room with Joss.

The highs and lows of music came from a speaker on the windowsill in Joss's room. The rest consisted of a mattress stained with fluids on the floor with only a top sheet. There was a large beanbag chair in the corner and some clothes hanging in a closet with no doors. Joss was spread out on the mattress wearing tiny booty shorts and a tank top. Her breasts were bulging out of the sides and her dark nipples pitching tiny tents against the shear yellow fabric. She pulled a pint of whiskey from the side of the bed and took a swig.

"Mouth wash." She said with a half grin but refused to look me in the eye.

I stood over her. "I saw you the other night."

"Yeah, it was my day off." She said and rolled her eyes up towards mine. When they connected, they grew large, and she sat up immediately and looked to the door.

I shook my head "no".

"Ah, fuck you dumb." She said with fear cracking her words. "I could scream."

"You won't."

"Or what you beat me up like you did T-bag?"

"No. I won't hit you." I said without moving.

Joss's brown eyes connected with mine. "T-bag is my boy; he takes care of me."

"No, he doesn't. This isn't care."

"What the fuck you know white boy? Probably just go around stealing and beating up people for money. And come here to beat off on little kids."

"Wrong. I came here looking for a single girl. Her name is Milo, and her family wants her home."

Joss looked away, down at the soiled bedroom floor. She took another swig of the bottle. "I ain't talking to you."

"I've got money and I can help you outta here, right now."

She turned to me again, her eyes glowing embers of fire that refused to die. "What makes you think I want to leave?" She stood upon the mattress, still a good six inches shorter than me. "Don't you get it? I can't leave, got nowhere to go. I'm trapped. Trapped in this life, in this room and trapped like you."

A teenage prostitute named Joss saw me for what I truly was. Something Sanford couldn't see and something Chloe didn't want to see. My mask was off with Joss, I was a criminal who hurt people to survive. Together we were trapped in a world without morals and that forced us to grow up too fast. All I was to this girl was a man who steals for his money, and truthfully, I am. Up until a few weeks ago I had never earned a paycheck in my life. Now I was trying to change and become something new, but the very next thing I did was go back to what I knew, to steal. This young teenager saw that in me even though I hadn't. The difference is, I found the hope to try.

"You can get out, you aren't trapped."

"Can we just do this, man." She pulled her kinky black hair back tight, tying it up.

"No, we can try."

She sighed, "You gonna take me outta here, past Kris?"

I held out my hand. She folded her arms and looked away.

"Na, you better just go. I won't tell." She continued to not look at me.

I peeled off a hundred bucks and set it on the mattress.

"You pay Kris." She said looking at me again.

"That's for you. I'll take care of him." I turned and started for the door.

"Wait." Joss stepped off the mattress and caught my shoulder. "I don't know for sure, but I think the girl you want is at another house, they keep 'em all over town. That little man you with, he know her. Try the house they use for kids that won't break."

She tried to hand me the cash back adding, "Keep it. If Kris finds I'm holding out he'll beat the hell out of me."

I smirked, "You don't have to worry about him." And pushed another hundred at her.

Images of the night in the back of the pool hall. The girl who ran from the glory hole and into the darkness could have been Joss. It could have been the girl in the room next to us. It could have been Milo. Delroy bragged about having a new gig, stealing the drugs was nothing to him. It was a mistake allowing T-Bag, Delroy and anyone else tied to this sex trafficking to live. I took their cash from drug deals. I gave it to people like Joss. It wasn't enough. I knew now what I had to give back. Violence. It was the only thing men like Delroy and Kris sitting in the other room knew. I knew it too. Violence I took and violence I would give back.

Sanford knew this when he assigned me this case. He wanted me to see this to the end. There is only one thing you can do when your house is infested with rats. I stepped into the hall and rounded the corner to the living room. Kris was leaning back in the rickety dining room chair watching TV.

"That ain't took long." He said without looking at me. I slipped my hand into my back pocket and came out with a curled brass fist and sunk it into his skull. Kris toppled over and spilled out onto the moldy carpet. His right arm went up in a hazy wave trying to fan off another hit, though I hadn't moved. His brain had just been rocked and was firing on all cylinders to catch up to what happened. His skull was cracked and bleeding. A long leg went out as he tried to stand but he just fell back down, still waving that arm thinking he was fighting me off. I grabbed him by the wrist and dragged him into the bathroom, dumping him in the tub. I stuffed a towel in his mouth and then ripped down the shower curtain and wrapped him in it. His eyes kept rolling, unable to fix a glare at me.

Joss was standing in her doorway when I walked out of the bathroom. She peered past me but said nothing. The other girl never came out of her room. I peeled off some more cash from the stolen wad and handed it to her.

"For whoever is in there if they'll use it." My expression was blank and so was hers. She was thinking of her next move, but nothing good came. I watched her turn back for the room only to turn around again. Lost in a world just given back to her and she was drowning in the sea of possibilities.

I reached for the wad of cash in my pocket, thinking more would help her get farther away from this place but it still didn't guarantee her safety. My fingers pinched the card Deputy Camp gave me. I handed it to her.

"Call her, tell her about all this. She's a good one you can trust," I said.

Joss looked at the card and then at me, "Shit, ain't no good cops."

"You want out? You want to break outta this cage? Call her, tell her to take you some place safe." I turned and headed for the door.

"There's still Luther out in the car." She said holding tightly to the green cash.

"You know that limp he's got, I gave it to him." I smiled and for the first time she smiled back.

I turned and headed for the door. She called behind me, "Go find her. Maybe she ain't gotta be trapped like us, not that one."

Outside an approaching storm pushed cooler air ahead. The gentle breeze kept the air flowing over my skin cool. Jinky was sitting on the hood of his car with his face buried in his phone. He was engaged, swiping, and tapping to *like* or *dislike* or whatever. Luther had his car door open enjoying the breeze as well. The music was softly bumping from the trunk as the highs in the doors popped.

Luther's large eyes shined white as he tracked me approach the car. I watched those eyes casually roll to the upper walkway of the building. He climbed out of the car and hobbled over to me without his cane. I turned and saw Joss standing at the railing.

Luther had quick hands and got a small semi-auto out and waved it in my face, "I know you, yeah I know you mutha fuka."

I didn't move. Jinky looked up and then jumped off the hood of the Scion. He walked around behind Luther disappearing behind the big man.

"Now you know how it gonna feel to get shot."

I straight kicked him in his wounded leg and the large man toppled over. He was too large to drag so I stomped his head on the concrete there in front of the apartment and in front of Jinky. I kept stomping until I could feel my socks squish like a wet sponge under my foot.

Jinky stood frozen, the only thing moving was his stammering jaw as he struggled to form words about what he was seeing.

I turned to him and lunged forward wrapping both hands around his neck and began choking him softly, slowly cutting of the air supply. He stumbled back, falling into the driver's seat of the black Impala with his legs still out. My arms reached into the car to continue to put the squeeze on him. Boney appendages stretched out; weak fingers scratched at my arms, but I wasn't letting go.

As his red face began to fill in with a deep purple I let up. He gasped for air between coughing spells. His wheezing was high pitched. I shoved him across the front seat to the passenger's seat and got in shutting the door behind me.

It was hot in the Impala, but I couldn't risk anyone seeing or hearing us. Jinky began to catch his breath, but he still couldn't talk. My fingers easily wrapped around his thin bicep to hold him in place.

I looked out, up at the second-floor apartment I just left. I saw Joss still standing there. She had not run or gone back into the apartment.

"Give me your phone." I said to Jinky and then squeezed his arm a little tighter. He handed it over with no struggle. I dialed Officer Camp.

"This is Officer Camp."

"Apartments on Bent Tree, you know it?" I tried to disguise my voice making it deep and rough.

"Who is this?"

"You know it or not?"

"Sure."

"There's a brothel being run out of the second-floor apartment and a dead man in the parking lot."

"Whoa, is this a joke? Tell me who this is."

"Just another wanna be cop. Listen, there's a young girl named Joss. She will tell you everything. Come quick before she splits." I ended the call. Jinky's phone immediately light up with a return call from Camp. I tossed the phone in the back seat.

I turned to Jinky, "I'm going to wait while you calm down. Then you are going to answer a few questions for me. Do you understand?"

"Yep," scraped out over his still closed throat. The color in his face and neck was a hot pink but would eventually return to the pasty white. I could see the white outline of my hands around his red pencil neck. It could have snapped so easily. I still might get my chance to do it, but first I need Milo.

"Milo Hines. Can you take me to her?"

The scrawny little punk swiveled his head without speaking.

"The house they keep the kids they can't break. You know it?"

This time he nodded yes.

"Take me there." I said as I turned the key to the Impala.

"Did you just call the cops on yourself?" Jinky said sitting up. "Like, who does that?"

We drove out of the parking lot.

<u>Chapter 10</u>

Trust was being tested. I had to go on trust that Joss wouldn't lead Camp straight to me. I had to trust Camp wouldn't turn me in and I had to believe if she did, Sanford was that good of a lawyer to keep me out of prison a second time. I had to go on trust if any of what I was doing would make a difference.

The cloud cover lowered, casting mist over the road, like the mist through my mind. 3rd Street was moving in on the underage sex slave business. Disrupting the dope trade was my guiding light that shown so bright I missed the sex being peddled in the shadows. Leaving them alive was a mistake I now had to correct. On my phone was the picture of the spreadsheet I took at DelRoy's office. The numbers and letters meant nothing but as I assigned arbitrary meaning, something started to emerge.

I drove not knowing where I was going, only relying on the silent gestures of Jinky. I didn't know what day it was or the time. It didn't matter, I was driving blind either way and I wanted to get Milo as soon as I could. Images creeped into my mind like the overweight middle-aged men creeped into her bed or the toilet stall next to her, breathing heavy with anticipation for her youngness to be shattered. It made sense to me now why Sanford wanted me to put an end to it. The knot in my stomach began to tighten. The anticipation for death grew.

"Here, turn here." Jinky pipped up. The voice from the cellphone advised the same. He pulled on his seatbelt as he sat up. His willingness to cooperate was improving. Still, every time I looked over at him it was with intent to kill him. He read between the lines in my face, his voice quivered with the next set of directions.

The roads were wet now, but the rain had stopped. Streetlights reflected circles of glowing yellow off black streets. Jinky punched away at his cellphone. I reached over and snatched it from his hands.

"Wait, I need that!" He said. "I need to let them know we're coming."

I screwed up, I had relaxed, and my guard had gone down.

The phone glowed in my face. Jinky reached out, trying to snatch it from me but failed. I switched hands from right to left holding the phone. Then threw my right palm into Jinky's face. His head popped back, bouncing off the tinted glass. He made a sore face and rubbed the spot on his head.

A text came through. It was as string of obscenities and abbreviations for them then, "NVM we got THIS!"

My foot fell harder on the accelerator, the six-cylinder pumped hard slinging the Impala, spinning the 22's all over the wet roads. I looked over at Jinky, "You're going to tell me what I'm walking into, or I kill you now. If, when we get there, it doesn't match up with what you describe, I kill you. Understand?"

Jinky crinkled his eyes and faked a sick smile trying to be cute, for a second, he didn't believe me. I hit the brakes on the car and slid the rear around bringing us to the other side of the road. Before the car even stopped rocking, I reached across the center console, grabbed Jinky by the neck and bashed his head against the dash. He squealed and put up his arms along the sides of his head to cushion the blows, but it only made me slam him harder.

The corner of his eye began to bleed. The blood mixed with his tears as he begged me to stop. I thought of how Milo might have begged for her captors to stop, so I rocked his head into the dash once more. After that I let go of him. I was breathing heavy through my nose, I was a bull eyeing red.

"Tell me what to expect."

Jinky was a smart punk who used his feminine frame to get out most fights, but I could tell this wasn't the first beating he had taken. Sniffling and wiping his nose then his eye, he said, "I've never been inside okay. The guy I go through is Uri, he'll take you to Milo. I gotta tell you man, you fucked up." His face twisted and more blood rolled from his busted eye as he smiled.

"Been that way my whole life."

"Well, these guys don't play. They're called *The Breakers* for a reason." Jinky's lip curled with excitement. He was enjoying the anticipation for what was to come. "I don't what you want with Milo, but I can tell you it isn't worth all this."

In 900 feet your destination is on your left.

We turned off a busy divided road onto a street I had never noticed was there. It was dark with no streetlights or sidewalks. Each side of the street was lined with thick Florida jungle you couldn't see two feet into during the day and nothing at night. It was as if the whole city had suddenly disappeared, and we traveled back in time before the racetrack and spring breakers. The last street of the way things was in old Florida.

A dim yellow glow through the trees led us to a cut away in the curb and a white crushed coquina road took us towards a wood frame house from the 1940's. The porch was screened but most of it torn or missing. The single yellow light, threw shadows of the bugs as they circled, daring each other to get closer. I parked the Impala. I waited for him to send a last text then we got out.

From the shadows of the porch the flash of a lighter lit up a dark man's face. His cigarette glowed red, bouncing as he made his way into the light. His long slender frame filled the doorway. He had on a baggy shirt and sagging shorts. A long drag of the cigarette illuminated his face once more. He had light skin and dark features. He waved us forward.

"You…you want a girl huh? A specific girl, eh?" Uri's accent matched his name, something from Eastern Europe. I didn't know from where and it didn't matter to me. I needed to find Milo and burn this place down. The texting between Jinky and this guy seemed routine, other than Uri upset we came out here to his secret dungeon. A place he kept the special ones, the ones that refused to be broken.

Uri looked past me to Jinky, his eyes squinting to make out the fresh bruise on the young man's face. "Jinky, what happen to face huh?"

Jinky said calmly with a shrug, "Teenage girls man." He even forced a smile that faded as he looked to me.

"I know a guy, Randall Brume. He recommended her." I said to Uri. Everything that happened with Kris and Luther happened fast. This was dragging out. To complicate things, in the dim light I couldn't see five feet past the edges of the house. I was exposed and unarmed. I had always operated under the cover of shadow and night. Now I was standing in the light, surrounded by shadow and empty handed.

"Yes, I know Randall. He would not have recommended this one. She, um she hurt him bad."

I said nothing.

"Maybe that's why you come, eh? You like the pain? Yes, I can see you do in your eyes."

Quiet on both sides, then I smiled, and he smiled, but neither one of us wanted to smile. He turned and led me up the uneven porch steps to the door. At the top, he stopped and looked back at Jinky, "Jinky, you come too."

He turned his back on us and entered the house with the confidence that we would do as he told.

Inside the place was hot. A ceiling fan spun and all, but one light bulb was out. The carpet was old and brown with swirl designs that were popular thirty years ago. I could feel fleas latching to my ankles and immediately begin feeding. A long sandy brown couch and matching chair were in the middle of the room. Beyond that was an eat-in kitchen. On the table was a tablet, ashtray and dirty plates and cups. Two chairs were pulled out and sitting in one was a guy in a blue tracksuit with white stripes down the legs. He had a shaved head and chubby round face. He sat smoking a cigarette. The tracksuit jacket was tight, and I could make the outline of a pistol tucked under his arm. His stare was blank, the head never moved.

Jinky was behind me and waved at the man, but he remained still.

"He's here for the rough stuff." Uri said and smiled to the man in the chair. Uri chuckled but the man did not. I eyed him but couldn't let it last too long. He had that fighter's gaze, he wanted me to challenge him eye to eye. The more I held it the more aggressive he would be. I forced myself to break it, look away. It was an act I hated myself for doing.

"She is a little, um, out of it at the moment. You know going through the treatment." Uri said using his fingers late to make air quotes. "So, if a fighter you want, um, maybe you spend money on Nicholai." He laughed alone.

"If I could just see how she is, maybe there's something to do with her." I forced a smile, "Randy, he said she's worth it."

I gnashed my teeth and barely got the words out. This undercover business was shit, playing along like a pedophile was getting under my skin. I knew being a P.I. would mean lying about who I was at times or why I was there but this, this was different. I had to look at it like a thief. I was there to steal Milo. It was the only way I could get through it.

Uri waved me on down the hall. We got to a closed door, and he said, "Here you are my friend." But did nothing to open it. I felt the hairs on my neck stand. I grabbed the handle and twisted.

Inside the room was pitch black. Immediately I felt the shove from behind. I chose to go with the momentum instead of resisting, but as I went, I went low. The waft of something solid whooshed over my head. I heard the ping of the aluminum bat imbed in the cracked plaster. The batter grunted as the vibrations went up both arms.

I stayed low and sprang out, opening my arms wide, closing them around the man's waist. We went down together but I was on top hammering away. The man grunted once more then went limp beneath me. I rolled off him and stayed low reaching out for anything in the blackness. I felt a wall and put my back to it just as the door burst open.

Nicholai stood, back lit from the hall, waving his pistol. He flipped a switch and sent light into the blackness.

I got my bearings as my eyes adjusted in time to see him find me. We were only a foot apart as our eyes met once more. He couldn't react fast enough as I grabbed at his weapon. His strength surprised me, forcing a double grip of his wrist. His free hand balled and came in for my face. I tucked my ear to my shoulder and let the top of my head take the brunt. His knuckles popped as they glanced off my scalp.

The pistol went off. With ringing in my ears, I drove a knee into his scrotum and then did it again. He didn't make a sound, but I knew he was in pain. I drove him back against the door, shutting it. He leaned on it to stay on his feet. Nicholai wasn't letting go.

Uri was banging on the door, but he was not strong enough to force it open.

Nicholai's free hand went back once more leaving his face exposed. The point of my head smashed into the bridge of his nose with such force that instantly my own eyes filled with his blood. The next moment I was holding his wrist up as his body slumped.

With Nicholai now limp, Uri charged through the door wielding a knife. He saw me holding Nicholai's arm and the other man on the floor. He uttered a few cusses in his native tongue and then joined the dance. The blade poked and slashed but did not taste my flesh. It did, however, force me to bounce back before I could get the gun from Nicholai's grasp.

Uri snickered as he dared me to come closer. Taunting me to go for the gun, he stepped back then lunged forward. We did this routine a couple times and I found my timing on the third try. Uri lunged in with a smile and I spun, kicking him in the side of the head. He dropped the knife and bounced as his body hit the floor.

My hand slid into my back pocket and came out wrapped in brass. These men hurt children. They took delight in their suffering. How they must have felt so powerful, their grown hands smothering over the smaller children. I went to work on Nicholai first. His smug face was quickly unrecognizable as the brass tore away the flesh and fractured the bone beneath. Awake or not, I beat him into eternity.

Then it was the batter. I worked him until my shoulder muscles ached with acid. They would be the ones broken now. Each of their faces I turned to lumps of dough. Uri began to stir from his blunt force stupor. His words slurred and his eyes couldn't catch a gaze. I stood over him, looking down on a beaten man who had done the same to so many. I hit him once more and he slipped into the blackness. I gathered their weapons and closed the door.

The other room in the house was empty of people, only the remnants of clothes too small for adults. I found Jinky outside trying to get in the Impala. His problem was that I held the keys. As I stepped off the porch, he froze. His eyes grew large with freight as he looked over my blood splattered neck, face, and arms. His shoulders tensed up; his face peeled back as his mouth opened in a silent scream. Someone else's blood dripped from my brass knuckles. Jinky broke into a flittering sprint. With no direction his legs tangled, and he fell.

I snatched him up and dragged him back, kicking all the way, to the car. The pistol was out and, in his face, now.

"Where is she?" I said.

Once he stopped stammering, he said, "I don't know. Really, I thought this was the place."

I slapped him with an open hand. He continued to deny knowing where Milo was until I put the brass knuckles back on. He eyed the blood, and the brass then came up with a story about seeing her two weeks ago. T-bag had called him and said Milo was giving him trouble. I imagined what inhumane shit they would do to break her. My guess was they bring her here for Uri and his goons to shoot her up and repeatedly rape her until she learned. I thought about the picture Gregg provided, how sweet and young she looked. Fuel for my hate.

I smacked Jinky hard this time and put him in the car.

I had to go back into the house, there was work left undone. Being a thief, I knew to check the hard-to-find spots, but the house was bare. The worn couch was flipped, and every cushion sliced open. Every closet was empty and checked for compartments. I checked the pockets of the dead. Their phones were cheap flip phones that held nothing but a couple of numbers. No buried information like on a smart phone; map, photos, apps to tell me where they had been or might go. Uri's phone I kept.

Uri came to while I was going through the phones. He rolled to his side and stared for a few seconds before finally piecing the last few moments back together.

"Ah, you no regular John I think." He said rubbing the burn mark my Vans made when it whipped across his face.

I knelt beside him and pulled Nicholai's pistol from my pocket, "You're going to tell me where you keep the girls, like the Milo girl."

Uri's smart-ass smile revealed bloody gums and a loose tooth. He pulled the tooth and spit the blood at me.

"Fuck you pig!" Uri snapped.

"You think I'm a cop? You get no phone call here; you have no rights with me. I'm going to cause you a lot of pain unless you tell me." I let the pistol do the rest of the talking and shot him through his foot.

Uri screamed and held the ankle of the dangling foot that now had a hole through it. He clenched his teeth and sucked deep breathes. The blood seeped from the wound and pooled on the floor. He rocked back and forth but refused to speak.

"I'll find her without you." I stood up and shot him through the knee of the other leg.

This time he did not hold back the wailing. He rolled around on the floor and yelled at me in Russian.

In the kitchen, under the sink, I found a can of paint thinner. I took Nicholai's lighter off the table and went back to the room.

Uri was laying on his back, blood drained from his body. He rolled getting on all fours and shook his head like a dog waking from a long nap.

The acid rose in my throat as my fingers slip through the brass rings on the knuckles.

The man looked up at me, his left arm reaching at my waist, his mouth opened but I slammed it shut with brass. Crooked yellow teeth spilled out of his mouth like a ripped box of Chicklets. The second time around the brass broke facial bone collapsing his eye socket. He flattened out his arms as his legs sprawled.

Uri's one eye was swollen shut; the other followed me as I poured the paint thinner on the bare mattress.

Uri started talking but none of it had to do with where Milo was. He didn't know, and it didn't matter much right at this moment. He was going to pay for his crimes, not for keeping quiet, but for ruining countless lives. His part in the sex trafficking world was over.

"Rats." I said as I pulled back on the lighter. Uri's hands went up, palms open, fingers spread wide, his mouth opened in a silent plea for me to stop.

I walked out of the house and was surprised to find Jinky in the car.

"What happened to Uri?" He asked.

The front room window began bellowing black smoke and then flames shot out, starved for oxygen, they climbed up into the night sky. The flames' roar drowned out the screams.

I spun the car around and drove out of there with the glowing orange blaze in my rearview mirror.

Chapter 11

The fire was set. The house of cards was in flames and soon the ashes would blow away in the salty breeze over the city.

We rode along in silence for a while with no real direction for either of us. At a stop light we watched two fire trucks blow through the intersection on their way to a house fire. My chest was still tight, and I thought about Uri's face, looking up at me with a defeated stare. These were bad men, and they will never do bad things again. It's what Sanford wanted and it's what I wanted now.

Joss's word, *trapped*, played over in my mind. Even when you get away with a crime, you are still tied to it. No matter the time and distance, you are never totally free. Every heist, every car, all of them have my fingerprints on them no matter how clean I scrubbed them. Sanford saw the criminal in me, as hard as I tried to hide it, he found it. As a criminal I had control of what I stole. I controlled the jobs I took. Killing was never one of them. Sanford drew me out, got me up to the line and baited me to cross it. And I did, of my own free will, becoming more trapped than I ever was. When this over, I will pay Sanford a visit about that.

I knew my next visit would be to T-bag. I had underestimated him. I took him for a scrawny low rung drug dealer, but he was more than that. I needed to be more prepared for my next encounter. I doubted Billy would have my back anymore. The way I left things between us I would be lucky if he even worked on my truck again. All these years we partnered together in high stress environments, trusting each other to sit on cash and jewelry or hot cars and not pull a double cross with a tip to the cops. I couldn't let it end that way.

We were on the beachside cruising along A1A. The ocean air and straight open road gave me time to think. Being a thief taught me a lot about being prepared for the job and to not take one unless I could get out clean. Billy was the best at it. He could steal a car and sell it right back to the owner with a smile, worry free. It came from the confidence in knowing the job. This world was new to me. I had only been a P.I. for a few weeks and now I'm killing people. I didn't think it should be this way.

It was getting late and the adrenaline from what I had just done was draining. My insides where twitching and I needed to just get out and walk around. I parked the Impala in front of a convenience store under the big spotlight the owner hoped would deter any criminals. We sat with the car off. Jinky hadn't moved or said anything since we watched the house burn down.

"I need something to drink." My voice escaped from my mouth in tired words. Jinky nodded. At this point he had nowhere to run, no safe places left. He was too complicit in the crimes of this sex ring to go to the cops and T-bag would probably kill him or worse. He was trapped the same as me. Without me he would be alone, looking over his shoulder. He knew either I would be there, or they would. His best bet would be to stick with me for now.

We grabbed energy drinks from the coolers and made out way to the counter. In the light, I could see Jinky's eye had stopped bleeding but there was still a rusty trail of dried and smeared blood down the side of his face. I could feel the bruises on top of my shaved head and figured by now they were a dark purple. The dried blood from the men I killed spotted my face and neck like chicken pox. My shirt was splattered as well. Our arms hung low, and our reaction time was a little behind as we paid for the drinks.

The clerk, a young, thin man behind the counter stared at us as blankly as we returned an exhausted blank stare. He said nothing of our bruises or blood stains. I gathered the change without a word.

The energy drink did its job, even if only temporarily. I was more alert and ready to get back to the investigation. I drove the car around the back of the convenience store. It was a nice dark place to talk. Behind the store was a small asphalt lot that ended with a berm of construction debris covered with sand and weeds. Beyond, a tall white fence securing a row of townhomes. From across the street, we could hear the ocean churning, pounding waves smashed the white sands erasing the tracks of the day's visitors. I pulled Milo's picture up on my phone. I showed it to Jinky.

"I'm going to find her and it's better for you if you help."

"Sure, but who is that, cause it's not Milo." Jinky let out that damn giggle.

"What do you mean? I got this picture from her father." I looked at the picture again. I zoomed in on her face. A girl about thirteen, freckles and brown hair, smiling enjoying what she had left of her youth.

"Man, I don't know who that is. Milo's not a kid, I can tell you that." Jinky giggled, this time at me and at the wool someone pulled over my eyes. He feared me less now, saw a flaw, and took pride in knowing something I didn't know. I should have smashed his face for thinking that, but I needed his cooperation and that meant for him being able to speak.

"But you do know Milo Hines?"

Jinky shrugged, "Yeah, I mean I know *a* Milo. The older Milo, I ran into her at the skating rink. I'd see her there talking to some girls. I thought she was one of the moms. I asked around because I didn't want her catching me talking to her kid or anything, you know. So, like that would be bad. But yeah, no, none of the girls said it was her mom."

His voice was high when he spoke about her. The five hairs on his chin had me convinced he wasn't over fifteen, but I knew better, at least I thought I did.

"How old are you?"

Jinky's know-it-all smile faded. "I'm in my teens, why?"

"Cut the shit."

"I just turned twenty, like a few months ago, okay." He went on to mumble into his drink can then took a long slurp.

I had so many questions for the pervert sitting next to me, but I had to play it close. He knew more than me and that was supremacy. The levers of power shifted; we were using each other right now but that could change quickly if he got the upper hand. Jinky was only cooperating to stay alive.

Staring into the picture of Milo, just a young teen standing in the yard of a nice suburban ranch home. I studied the young face then moved on to inspect the clothing. The denim suspenders, the multiple bracelets on her wrist, and bright white Keds. I wasn't up on fashion by any means, but I knew cars and that '92 Lincoln Town car in the driveway of that ranch style home was way too shiny and new to be well preserved car. Greg Hines was a wealthy lobbyist. There was no way he drove old cars and dressed his kid in hand-me-downs.

"So how old would you guess Milo is, the one you know?" Rust broke from the wheels in my tired mind.

"Like thirty something. Great body, nice tits." His hands went out to mimic the cups.

We sat in silence finishing our drinks. Once the cans were empty, I said, "Okay, time to spill it. Tell me all of it."

Jinky looked over at me, "Or what?"

"You either tell me or you don't. You have a choice right now. Help me tear this thing apart or I turn you lose, but you better start running. When I'm done with Milo and T-bag and all the other child pimps and perverts, I'll come for you."

Jinky's brow wrinkled as his thoughts blotted out what he was actually seeing. Instead, he was seeing in his mind what I didn't say I would do, torture, maim, and kill. His imagination scared him more than any threat I could make.

"Yeah, yeah you got it."

"Good. Tell me about your part in all this and just what *this* is."

Jinky spilled it and I believed him. He went all the way back, back to elementary school and how he was labeled a pervert then and the names his mom called him and a lot of bullshit I didn't need to hear but it relaxed him as he got it off his chest. Finally, he got to what I needed to hear.

Jinky explained how he had a knack for talking to young girls and they would follow him around. He began a cult like status as girls wanted to know him. Soon, if they were texting him sexual things it was a prestige thing at their junior high. Kind of like dating the quarterback he claimed, though I couldn't see it. Eventually the girls would send nude pictures and he would black mail them all the while introducing them to drugs. Mostly prescription pills because it would knock them out and when they came to, he told them they had sex, even if they didn't.

It was difficult to hear and Jinky was detailed. I wanted to ball my fist and pound his testicles into dust. I didn't, I let him continue.

Jinky was approached by this Milo lady one night while leaving the skating rink. She quickly turned the tables on him and convinced him one of the girls was going to talk and spill it all. The only way out was to get the talkative girl drugged up and take her to a safe house Milo had. She described it as a place the girl would learn to accept things and be okay with them. She had several of these houses around town and they weren't always the same, locations changed often. He finished his story, with not knowing how T-bag was connected or why and that he hasn't seen Milo in weeks.

"I didn't know about all this locked up shit man, I swear." He said crinkling the empty aluminum can.

"What did you think was going on? You're not that stupid, Jinky."

Jinky blinked a few times then said in a quiet nearly whispered tone, "I guess I just didn't want to think about it. I refused to."

He stared out the window towards the field. I let him think about it now. I hoped he was picturing all their young faces and how he ruined their lives because of the hell he claimed happened to him at that age. I hoped his stomach churned and smashed like the ocean just across the street, pounding the sand, erasing the past. I wanted to see him puke, I wanted to see him die.

Jinky's hand went for the door handle. I didn't move to stop him, instead waited for the young man's decision. Slowly he let go and tucked the hand under his leg.

"Milo is dangerous. People who cross her don't ever do it again because they disappear. Like straight up never seen again. Not just the kids, like parents too. Anyone who questions gets erased. I don't want to be erased like that."

"Then do something," I said.

He nodded.

"I never liked T-bag. He picked on me in high school. You know his real name is Clarence." And Jinky giggled to himself.

I knew Jinky a little better now. I started the car and we headed out.

Chapter 12

Sitting beside your own shallow grave sends you on a long trip deep into your soul. Coming that close to death changes a man, realigns what is important and points the arrow true north to the ones you can trust. I trusted him now that he faced death and came back with the grit to fight.

T-bag would not leave himself open like when I found him a few nights ago. He was a shark then swimming around with no one to challenge his bite. I've never thought of myself as a whale, but you can call me Shamu, the killer whale, the only thing out there eating sharks.

That same electricity that was surging through the crowd of middle schoolers was working its way up my spine as I anticipated another go at T-Bag. We cased his apartment, and it was lights out empty. The rush was subsiding, and I needed it to continue. Jinky got on the phone and asked around, but no one was giving up his location. It was becoming clear T-bag was in hiding.

The night went on and I had no solid lead on T-bag. My fingers gripped the steering wheel pressuring my brain to come up with a direction to find answers. Pain emanated from swollen knuckles making my hands feel weak. Another energy drink would not get us any further, so I headed back to the skating rink. Jinky reminded me his car was at the apartment where I beat two guys to death, and I told him that's why I was dropping him at the rink. He could get his car in the morning.

Jinky stood with the car door open but didn't say anything. He started a few times but never made out a full word. Finally, I asked him what he wanted to say.

"I just, I want to help." Jinky's voice cracked. It could have been exhaustion or genuine sadness.

"Okay, start by letting me know if you hear anything."

"No, more than that. I want to do more than that. I want to find Milo. Maybe that will take some of this away."

"Some of what?"

Jinky curled his lips back into a smile then let it fade quickly, "This pain." He shut the door and walked towards the rink that had long ago closed for the night.

I was a mixed bag as I drove away. My own churning had subsided for the night leaving me with calmer thoughts. There was a sense of something good coming out of this dark, cold place I had run straight in to. I wanted Jinky to face justice for his crimes but tonight his own judge delivered him a guilty verdict and he began serving his sentence tonight. He was given three life terms, life of guilt, life of hurt and a life of pain for what he had done. I wondered about my own sentence.

****

The couch had no comfortable positions left for me as I flopped from one position to another. I listened to a garbage truck dropping an empty dumpster behind my building. It was mid-morning and the weight of the night before sunk my shoulders. The blood of other men had dried and caked under my nails in the tiny crevasses of my skin. I dragged myself to the can, licked my wounds and came back searching for coffee. It took two cups before I caught my reflection blanky staring out the window.

Luther's labored breathing and Kris's confusion as he suffocated in the tub filled my ears and kept my eyes from shutting. Guilt and regret were too small to feel, it was something else bothering me. I did what had to be done and now I forced them away, pushing them ever smaller in my mind until I could no longer see their faces. It wasn't the body I killed, it was the evil they did that I killed last night, and that gave me peace.

I forced images of Chloe to pass the time. I had avoided her for so long and she really wasn't that bad. She was attractive, successful and her kid enjoyed spending time with me. There was an instant family waiting for me. To make a family work, I would have to put the criminal world away for good. I punched out a text but deleted it, then did it again but deleted that too. The desire to see her was only to avoid the pain I had amassed. Pushing away the killing and turning to her for escape was wrong, it was unsustainable.

Jinky had no leads on Milo, only a sneaky curve ball that had me thinking Milo was a grown woman. I have heard of madams and women running brothels, but a child sex ring? As Uri and his partners burned, the Milo I was after was farther away than ever.

I decided to make a few calls to unload the Impala before the cops found it. As soon as I described the car, everyone backed off. I had no other choice but to call Billy and grovel. If I was lucky, I would get out of it with a lecture on where I went wrong. The way I left things the other night would not be working in my favor. There was a chance he wouldn't help.

The phone rang and rang. I got his voice mail. I called again and again and again. I sat back rubbing my temples. Then he called back.

There was silence on both ends then he finally spoke, "Yeah?"

"I've got to take a dump." It was an old, coded message we came up with years ago, when dick and fart jokes ruled our humor pallet. I came up with this one time when I had to call him about a car, we needed to get rid of and I hadn't found a buyer yet. The car was 1972 Mustang Cobra Jet. She was something special because of some mods Carol Shelby did himself to the car, I didn't care at the time. The heat was on me big, and I freaked out about wiretaps and tried speaking in code. The old memory plus the fact it was still funny must have struck a chord because Billy stayed on the line.

"Okay." I could hear Billy's smile through the phone. He wanted to laugh but fought it.

"*Okay* I can shit at your place or *okay* I gotta go find my own shitter?"

"Do we really have to talk about your shit?" Billy lost the smile in his voice. I was pushing it close to the line.

"Probably not." I said sullenly.

He breathed heavy into the phone and said, "Do you want to describe your stool to me?"

I laughed alone, "Black. I took a dump a few blocks down. Didn't flush it." I snickered again.

"Dude, we're gonna have words when you're done with all your shit." Billy hung up.

I sat back in the chair wondering how he would know which car he needed to dump. Somehow, he would pick it out, take it someplace and it would be gone forever. He used to say he was channeling his Cherokee ancestors who were the best horse thieves in their day.

A text had come through while I was on the phone from Chloe saying "Hi" and then another followed asking if I wanted to meet for brunch. Cooper's was putting on a monthly brunch and she would be there. I argued with myself and conceded that seeing Chloe was better for me than not seeing her.

I walked into Cooper's wearing my usual t-shirt and shorts and put my sunglasses on top of my head. I waited for my eyes to adjust before walking in further. A buffet was set up in the back and a line of people waited for more eggs to come out. I spotted Chloe with a brunette everyone would call cute, but I wasn't seeing it. All I saw was Chloe looking back at me with the same anticipation I had for her. They sat at a table with two empty chairs. I snaked my way through the tables to theirs.

"Roger," Chloe said raising a mimosa glass. She smiled tightly smile then said, "This is Anne. Have a seat."

I smiled and nodded to Anne who had a girl next door quality that everyone enjoys; evenly curled chestnut hair and smile with dimples you could lose a finger in. Her sun dress was tight and long, same as Chloe's. I looked around and found nearly all the women dressed identically. Each dress had a similar pattern with bright colors. Much of the men accompanying them were dressed in pastel colored button ups and boat shoes. I felt a little under dressed but this was my bar, they could all get the hell out.

The waitress stood over me and said the buffet was fifteen bucks and ten more for the unlimited mimosas. When she asked if I wanted an oatmeal stout, I looked up to see Alysa looking down at me. She forced a quick smile in case a manager was watching, and then held a pen to a notepad.

I smiled back, "Yeah, I'll take the stout."

She walked off.

"No breakfast?" Chloe asked munching on some bacon.

"I'm not that hungry."

"Oh, so you just came for the good company." She smiled and her friend smiled.

As I chuckled along with them, I wondered why I was there. I had formed a deep attraction to the hot mom I had lived next door to, but this just wasn't my scene. I felt embarrassed to have Alysa see me here at this hour, eating brunch with two broads in sun dresses. My eyes roamed and wandered finding rest upon a TV airing a local news broadcast. It was a familiar scene, outside the apartment complex I was at last night. They had a tarp up were I left Luther and yellow tape all over the second-floor apartment.

"Can you believe this shit?" Anne said between sips of her mimosa.

"Unreal." Chloe added as she too enjoyed the breakfast libation.

I said nothing, knowing a car belonging to the dead man on the TV was parked a few blocks away. I had been too tired to dump it in a swamp, but I did swap tags and wipe it down. Now I had to hope Billy got to it before the cops.

The news went on to the house fire that was still being investigated but as of yet unrelated to the two murders. Again, the girl's chimed in with their disbelief at the garbage in this town. This time Chloe added that her real-estate firm had just listed the house and added that it must be squatters in there trying to cook a meal that started the fire. She went on to say the same thing happened last year in an empty house that killed two runaway teenagers.

I couldn't fight my body's natural reaction to an explosion of ideas, as my eyes went large, and mouth fell agape. Chloe looked at me blinking but not saying a thing.

"When last year?" I asked as casually as possible, forcing my heart rate to level out.

"I don't know." Her eyes rolled to the upper corner as she thought and then came back to me with, "Early fall I think."

Alysa arrived with my dark stout. She asked if I wanted the buffet and I told her it would have to wait. I guzzled the stout faster than a stout should. My mind was set on the news report and what Chloe said about the house having been listed and the similar empty house with the dead teenagers.

I smiled and nodded at things the two women discussed, but I couldn't take the chit-chat and laid down a twenty once the last of the stout was gone.

"Out so soon?" Chloe said with a genuine frown on her face. Even then it was inviting, I wanted to correct that into a pleasurable smile for her.

"Sorry, I have an appointment."

Chloe turned to Anne, "Roger is a private investigator. Maybe he's working on the murder case." Chloe turned and pointed her sharp featured face toward mine. "So how about it, Roger, what's the case?"

I grinned out of the corner of my mouth, "Client privilege and all."

"A quiet secretive kind of man, aren't you Roger?"

I nodded and headed for the door.

Just outside the doors to Cooper's Alysa caught me.

"Hey," she said, spinning me on my heels.

"Yeah?"

"Here's your change." She held out $14.00.

"Keep it." I said and turned back to the street, but she caught me again.

"Hey,"

"Yeah?" I was getting annoyed; this girl had a special skill that luckily few in my life have and that is to annoy me. All the others with such a skill have been weeded out.

"Thanks. Now let me give you a tip,"

I said nothing, waiting for her to get out whatever she deemed so important.

"Watch yourself with that one in there. She's a destroyer of worlds." She put the cash into her apron. Her smile was round and there was a glint in her green eyes as she warned me with knowledge only other women held. She took a step back without turning and I wanted to reach out and pull her near me, thank her for the warning though I wouldn't heed it.

I watched her go, unable to come up with the words to make her stay. As I headed back to the office, a flurry of words and phrases flooded my mind. All of it was for another time, another meeting.

I needed to have a beer and think about it.

Back in my office, the first suds went down quick, so I opened another. This time I poured a shot of whiskey in it. Going through my contact on my cell was useless. The problem with being a loner who only works in a two-man team created a short list for contacts. For a guy who liked to gamble on the side, I hadn't played these odds well at all. A few weeks of training and a government stamp wasn't enough to keep me from getting in over my head. I wanted to be above board, to do a job and not watch my back for Johnny law, all of it so I could come out of hiding. The private investigator ticket was supposed to get me on track, to apply skills I had but bring them into the light, I was done working in the dark. Somehow all that was thrown back in my face. That teenage prostitute, Joss, was right, I was trapped in this life.

I got started on my third whiskey and beer.

My life had always felt free, I never clocked in and out, wore a suit or had a boss. I lived on the next score being the big one, and early retirement. Billy and I would hit the Metropolitan Museum of Art, heist a Degas or ancient pottery from the Shang Dynasty. It didn't happen. I thought I could just cut and run anytime, I tried the Army and still I returned to this life. Every direction I took to get distance between me and stealing was halted and back I came to the life. I wanted off this not-so merry go round.

Pope knew who I was way back then, and he offered me something Billy never did, Pope offered me a choice. Billy only offered another job, another chance to get caught. He made it sound like freedom, but he was just as trapped as I was. With every job we stepped one foot closer to that prison cell. Billy made it through with never more than the usual suspect rousing by cops. I was not the lucky one and did my time and never wanted to go back. Things never came easy to me without hard work. Swollen knuckles and lumps on my head were proof enough.

A knock at my office door got me out of my chair. I stood up and held the desk to catch my feet. The world spun a little faster. Unfazed, I walked a wavy line to the door.

Chloe was standing there in her long sun dress and a to-go box from brunch.

"You left without eating. I thought you might be hungry."

I took the food and she let herself in. I plopped back into my desk chair and started eating French toast with my hands. I paused to look at Chloe who had taken a relaxed seat on the couch. She looked over at the empty bottles.

"Day drinking alone, you might have a problem." Her smile said she wasn't concerned about my habit. She added, "You aren't alone now, so problem solved."

Chloe stood up and wandered lazily over to my refrigerator. She bent over and opened the small door, allowing the hinge of the door to transfer her hips side to side. She pulled a soda can and popped it open. After slurping the fizz, she sat on the corner of my desk. "I'll need a chaser." She said and lifted the whiskey bottle to her lips.

It was a long pull on the bottle. Her face nearly imploded as she sipped the soda to alleviate the burn.

She let out a *whoooaaa* and kicked off her wedge sandals, sending them thudding to the floor.

I grabbed the bottle from her, took a swig and kicked off my shoes as well.

"So, tell me private eye, what's the hot case you got now?" She tucked her feet under her as she curled up on my couch. A few strands of her hair were wild and free from the tightly pulled back bun. She ran her fingers over the wild ones trying to get them back in line. Eventually she gave up and winced as she gave up on the bun and let her long blonde hair fall over her shoulders.

"Missing cat," I said. She spread her fingers out as she ran them through the disheveled hair. It gave her a wild look, the way it would after several days on a deserted island. Just the two of us in the sand and the sun, no one around for miles. She was here now, keeping her buzz fed on my whiskey.

"I never knew you to chase pussy." She muted her laugh with her hand.

We broke eye contact and fell into silence. I sipped on my beer while she sipped the soda.

"Another shot?" she said getting to her feet then leaned on the desk. She grabbed the bottle and tilted it back then handed it to me.

"I was hired to find a missing girl."

"Kidnapped?" She settled back in the couch and cupped her chin in her hand.

"Runaway. I think she is caught up in the sex trade."

"Here in Daytona!" Chloe leaned forward with her hand out. I passed the bottle back to her for another swig.

"I see the prostitutes, walking daily up and down Ridgewood Ave, and I asked myself, how'd they get to that point? How'd they go from daughter, sister, mother to selling themselves on the street?"

Chloe handed the bottle back. I put the cap on, I was done drinking.

"Maybe they like it." Chloe shrugged. "I don't know."

"Adults, I don't care how they spend their time. What I found were girls, young girls. Joss, a real pro at fifteen. To be that cool and confident didn't happen overnight. She'd been at it awhile. That's the kind of organized abuse going on in this town right under our noses and Milo is lost in it somewhere. I've got to find her." My hand was a clenched fist.

"I'm sure you're doing your best." Chloe got up and moved to the desk. She was leaning against it, close enough for me to smell the organic oils of her shampoo.

I pointed the bottle at her and said, "Do you know who the realtor was in charge of the house that burned?"

Chloe's smile was empty, nothing but a way to stall while the wheels in her head spun. She wanted to change the subject, move on to the reason she was here.

"Not off the top of my head. I'm not even sure we managed that one."

"You think you can find out for me what company it was and who managed it and if there are anymore out there that are empty?" I took a second swig and passed the bottle back. Five shots and three beers in, I was starting to feel my blood thin. My brain was awash in whiskey and the case was losing importance. The girl in front of me was the only thing that made since right now.

She put the bottle down without drinking.

Her eyes narrowed, "So that burned up house *does* have something to do with this case. I knew you couldn't keep a secret from me Roger."

I smiled, my cheeks flushed with blood and alcohol, "Sure I can doll."

"Oh, no sir. I've studied your face for far too long." She drew closer to me, inches. I could smell whiskey and a bit of citrus on her lips. It wasn't close enough, I wanted inside.

*****

I woke up on the couch. My stomach was sick, and my head had been sawed in four places. I stood against the judgement I had long ago lost. Once my balance returned, I went to the window. Outside, the sun had dipped behind the building casting a long dark shadow across Beach Street. The ballpark already had their lights on but there was no game.

After staring out the window watching a street void of cars and pedestrians, I realized I couldn't remember anything after leaving Cooper's. I forced pieces of the day together, who I talked to and when.

Still images with no sound flickered in my mind, slowly building one on top of the other until I had a film reel sputtering through the day's events. Chloe was there. So was whiskey. Her shoes came off and so did my shorts. Her dress was up around her waist as she startled my lap. It spread out over the two of us, making modest of what went on underneath.

Images sped up adding movement to her lips, but I didn't know the words she spoke. I replied not knowing what I said. There was no piecing it together. Never had I drank to the point of blacking out and not remembering with some quickness, what happened the night before. This was different, it felt deeper, calmer and my head hurt in different places. My black out didn't feel normal.

I knew I had contacted Billy, so I went over my text messages. The texts eventually lead to a phone call. I didn't remember all the pieces to the call and what was said, but I had the impression it was fine. There was another call in the log I didn't remember making at all.

In my call log there was a missed call from Jinky and then a return call a minute later that lasted nearly three minutes. There was no memory of that, no image of answering, no whisper of a voice, nothing. It was like I never spoke to him.

I hadn't. Looking closer at my phone I noticed a dusky sheen smeared across the black mirrored finish of my phone. I swiped the oily residue with my finger and rubbed against another finger.

My distended belly rumbled, and I had to purge some of the alcohol. I slipped the phone in my pocket and hurried to the end of the hall.

After ending the unnatural call of nature, I sat, swiping through news articles on my phone. The cops had no arrests and they still had not found the black Impala. Officer Camp was mentioned as discovering the prostitution ring. The residue on my phone was building up on my finger and I wiped it with a square of toilet paper. The color came off an orangy-flesh color. I looked closer. I knew this color; I had seen it up close.

I finished what I started and burst out of there nearly forgetting to wash my hands. Back at my office I grabbed my tablet and opened it up. There were confidential files open as well as my email. The contents of my desk drawers had been shuffled. I dressed into fresh clothes and headed out.

It was a Sunday evening and the parking lot behind my building was empty. Much of Beach Street was a ghost town. The shops were closed, and everyone had gone home. My truck sat parked alone. As I crossed the lot, I needed to check on the Impala.

"It's gone." Billy answered.

"I owe you."

"Well, not as much as you think. You want to stop by?"

"Yeah, I'll head over now. I can catch you up on things in person."

He said OKAY and hung up. The phone slipped into my front pocket and that is when I noticed my waist felt loose, I had forgot my pistol. I had to head back to the office to grab my Glock. They knew who I was and that I was on to them, fists wouldn't be enough the next time we met.

Climbing the stairs, I spotted two guys in the hall, both wore sagging pants and large t-shirts. More importantly they were hanging near my office door.

My heart rate quickened as did my pace. They looked like 3rd Street members to me but everyone these days wanted to look like a gangbanger.

Just feet from my office door I heard a man ask for office 214. I turned and that's when I felt the sting of 100,000 volts race through my nervous system, clenching my muscles, scrambling my brain until I tipped over hitting the tile floor.

I looked up, still frozen, still fighting the electricity, to see a gaunt faced man in a sweatshirt zap me once more. After that I just stopped fighting it.

I could do nothing as they hurriedly bound my feet and hands. I floated away in their arms as I was dragged down the stairs and lifted into the back of a SUV.

My body tingled as thousands of tiny electric needles circulated through every muscle in my body. I heard my cell phone ringing. I watched as the passenger silenced the phone.

"Yo, man turn that shit off already." Said the driver and man who hit me with a stun gun, twice.

"I can't. She said she would call on his phone remember?"

The driver nodded but said nothing.

I pulled on the zip ties around my wrists and ankles. They were thick and cut into my skin as I pressed against them for freedom. I felt over my pockets, and they had been picked clean. My knife and wallet were gone.

That took the last effort from my over worked brain. I laid there in a daze not caring about escape or where they were taking me. I just wanted the tingling to go away. The less I thought about anything, the easier it was on my body. My consciousness floated away.

It was impossible to tell how long we drove around but eventually we stopped. The door opened and the passenger grabbed me in the armpits and dragged me out. He more so dropped me onto the dirt ground. I spit sand and roll to my side to get a good look around.

A thin pine forest surrounded a tan doublewide mobile home. A cloud of mosquitos hovered overhead. One by one they sniffed me sweat out and began divebombing to feast on my blood. There was nothing I could do to defend against them, bound and laying on the ground they drank.

Each man grabbed me under the arm and dragged me up the wooden porch, scraping my knees and shins along splintered boards, and into the house.

The lights were on but there was no furniture. The floor was carpeted to the open kitchen with no appliances. They worked together to prop me up against the north wall of the living room. The driver went down the hall to a back bedroom and came back out dragging a small-framed body.

Into the light, I could see it was Jinky. The bruises on his face I gave him were now a yellowy-blue. There were fresher bruises of deep red and purple. Dried blood caked his limited mustache hair. His nose was crooked.

He dropped Jinky next to me. I nodded and Jinky just looked at me then to our captors. The two men who brought us here stood without saying anything. Then T-bag made his entrance.

T-bag's fingers were taped where I broke them. He walked in with a bounce in his step and his lower lip protruding out trying desperately to look tough. I only thought of how I had made him cry.

"Well, well, well … happy to see me again?" He puffed on a blunt.

"Hello Clarence."

That took the *thug* off his face for a second. He moved in real close to my face and spit. The warm loogie rolled down to the corner of my mouth. He flung his loosely laced high-tops at me, kicking my ribs and one to my face. The kicks were light but connected. A knee came flying at my face, I heard my nose pop before I felt the pain and the warm blood seep out.

"Bitch." T-bag said slightly out of breath from beating me. He puffed out his chest. I strained hard on the ties. I was stuck. The driver had his stun gun. They stood just behind T-bag, flanking either side of him. I didn't see a weapon in the passenger's hand, but someone must have a pistol. It would be insulting if they didn't. Jinky kept his head buried, chin to his chest.

"You mutha fuckas done fucked up my bidness." T-bag was in full *gangsta*-swing with his hands moving like a marionette. He reached back to his waist and there was the pistol.

"Now I gots-ta kill you two." The barrel of gun waved back and forth from my face to Jinky's.

He paused waiting for us to beg or be defiant. Jinky and I stayed quiet. I kept my eyes on him.

My phone kept ringing.

"I said turn that shit off," the driver said to the passenger.

"Not till she call man."

T-bag snatched the phone and ended the ringing. "Milo said to call her from his phone, so she knew we got him, you dumb..." He mumbled the insult as if tired of creating new insults for the man. T-bag dialed out a number.

"Yeah, we got him. Yeah, the other one too. Okay." T-bag tossed the phone on the counter that separated the living room and kitchen. I spotted my wallet and knife. He turned to his men, "I'm gonna meet Milo and we're gonna settle this thing with Delroy, you know what I'm sayin'."

They nodded.

"So, finish this shit up and text me when you out." T-bag turned and got really close to my face again with the pistol shoved under my nose. I smelled gun oil.

"I wish I's the one gonna kill you fucka. But your Casper ass ain't worth my time."

I laughed, "It's ironic, your name being T-bag, because you don't have the nuts to do it."

I got kicked repeatedly for that remark. It worked out though. While on my side I scraped a protruding nail that was holding in the baseboard. It was sharp so I got the zip tie on it and slowly went to work. Each time I scraped the plastic tie over the nail I had to move, snort or cough to cover the sound. Each scrape took a little more but there was no way to tell just how much.

T-bag withdrew the pistol and walked back to the counter. My phone rang again. He smashed the pistol down on my phone then turned to his men and gave orders to kill us then bounced, leaving the gun on the counter next to my smashed phone. Standing in a long silence, the two looked to the other to go first. Jinky stirred from his frozen state.

"Derick," Jinky said talking to man I called Passenger. "C'mon man don't do this. I didn't do anything. It's not my fault." His eyes reddened and tears began rolling down.

My phone kept ringing.

"You messed up Jinky. You brought this on you man."

The driver said, "Turn that damn phone off! And take him outside."

"Me? You take him outside mutha fucka."

"I ain't about to leave this one here alone."

"So, we do him first stupid." Derick said getting in the driver's face. They shoved each other. Derick got a hefty one in and sent the driver into the counter. I watched my folded pocketknife slide off the edge and fall silently into the plush carpet.

The driver pulled out the stun gun. Feeling empowered he gave the order again. "I said take him outside or I will take you outside."

Derick breathed heavily, curled his fists then marched over and grabbed Jinky by the arm lifting him to his feet. The skinny guy was all tears with a heaving chest as he stood. Derick reached down and cut the zip ties around Jinky's ankles then shoved him towards the door.

Derick held out his hand, "Yo, give me the gun."

"No. Use the shovel."

"Nah, man, gimme the gun." Derik said louder. His eyes were on the counter.

"You better get out there." Driver lifted the stun gun.

Derik swore under his breath as he dragged Jinky towards the door. Jinky pleaded with his executioner as they exited the trailer.

It was just the driver and me. The blood flow from my nose dried, but my side still hurt from the kicking. I took a deep breath, it hurt like hell.

The driver glared me up and down, working up the nerve to take my life. Needing more confidence, he went to the window to watch his partner execute Jinky. The pretend kid was about to get what he probably deserved. I wasn't the one pulling the trigger on him but felt responsible. I didn't want Jinky to die but now wasn't up to me. My job wasn't over. I had to get to Milo and tear down the whole damn thing, Jinky included.

He came back and said, "Get on your feet."

I hadn't finished cutting the zip tie. I didn't know how much was left before I could break free.

"You'll have to stand me up." I said and gestured with my shoulder to help to lift me. As he leaned in, I head butted him hard. He staggered back and sat down on his ass. I pulled hard trying to separate my hands to break free. With a snap, my arms flung out to my sides.

I squatted then frog leapt towards the counter, landing on my side near my knife. My ribs burst into flames, but I had to keep moving. Rolling I grabbed the knife and flicked out the four-inch serrated blade. Driver got up, shaking off his daze. He roared and came at me with the stun gun out.

Driver's momentum had him barreling down on me. His eyes flashed as he saw my blade coming around. He swung his hand with the stun gun, going for my side but I dropped my left arm as the 100,000 volts charged through me. Just as the stun gun contacted my arm, I shoved the blade deep in his gut. We were linked, the charge holding my arm taught, volts racing through my muscles down the blade and into his guts.

He lay on top of me, his mouth open, drool seeping out. He didn't move or make a sound. I rolled to my side, and he toppled off taking the stun gun with him. My left arm was pins and needles again, but I still managed most of my faculties. I took the bloody knife and cut the ties from my ankles.

Driver was staring up at the ceiling, blood bubbling out of the wound just below his sternum. His eyes were wide as if he was watching a beautiful ballet. He gurgled and turned his head to see me with his fixed stare.

I gathered my wallet and the pistol and stood over him. He tried to swallow some of the blood coming from his mouth but choked instead. He wasn't coming back from this one.

Looking out the window, the sun was almost gone sending the sky into a purple decent as it covered the earth. I saw the shape of a man fifty yards away, at the edge of a pine tree forest. In his hands a shovel in motion, slinging dirt from one place to another.

I walked straight at him. He kept on shoveling without looking up until I was twenty feet away. There was a quick double take. Then he said, "Shit."

I fired twice hitting him in the chest. He fell over.

From where I was, I could hear the sucking chest wounds. He was laying three quarters on his right side. His left hand was extended out over his head still grasping the shovel. A few of his fingers twitched on his right hand.

The pistol was out and trained on him as I came up over his head. I put a foot on the shovel and fired twice more into his back. He died.

The pistol was wiped down and tossed in the woods.

From where he was shoveling, the earth began to shift then came a high-pitched wheezing. There in a shallow grave, covered in a few inches of dirt was Jinky, still bound at the wrists. His neck was doing all it could to keep his head up. Dirt covered most of his face.

I took a knee and drove my hand into the freshly tossed earth, felt around for his arm, and yanked him out of the grave. Sitting up, Jinky drew a massive breath and coughed between sniveling. Tears had made small mud balls down his cheeks, and he spit dirt. A snot bubble infused with dirt popped from his nose. He leaned into me with his head on my chest and wept silently.

I cut the zip ties from his wrists. Jinky rubbed his fresh wounds caused by the ties and then slowly curled into a tight ball. He sat next to his own grave, heaving and jerking, working to catch his breath. After a minute he began to calm down.

"Why didn't Derick kill you?"

Jinky sniffled then said, "The whole walk out he kept apologizing. He whacked me with the shovel, and I came to while he was covering me with dirt." His mouth opened again, lips pulling back over dirt covered teeth. No sounds came out only heaving again.

"I hate her." He said over and over.

"Why does Milo want you dead, Jinky?"

He repeated *"I don't know"* several times. I cut him off and asked how he got to the trailer.

"I got a call from her. She said she needed help, that there was heat on her and she wanted me to talk to some girls. It wasn't out of the ordinary. A girl gets spooked by what Milo asks her to do and I come in and smooth things over." He wiped the snot and muck from his face before continuing, "She sent T-bag to pick me up. He drove me out here and tied me up. Then you showed up."

There was a connection Milo found between Jinky and me, but who had eyes on us? The only people that saw us together were dead.

"Did you tell anyone you were with me last night?"

He shook his head no. I believed him, there was no reason not to. He was too deep to run his mouth, but nevertheless, Milo knew. Her feelers stretched far, and she had eyes everywhere. It was time I met this mythical beast face to face.

"Let's go." I stood up and started walking back to the house. Jinky got up and followed behind me.

Outside a breeze rustled through the pines bringing a cool dryness to my sweat covered skin. I broke out in goose bumps down each arm. It was quiet, almost peaceful minus the contorted body of the guy I just shot.

Jinky asked if I was going to burn this place down like I did the other house. I looked at him and then the mobile home and shook my head no and we headed back into the trailer.

The driver was dead on the floor. The blood had pooled on his chest but managed to stay there soaking into his shirt instead of the carpet. I went through his pockets and took his keys. Jinky asked if we should bury him. I decided to just leave him.

I made a sweep inside the mobile home. It was empty except on the counter was a sign in sheet from a realty company. The sheet had names of realtors on it, and I had overlooked it several times. I glanced at it once more and spotted a familiar name. She was here yesterday at 10:30 am.

We got in the SUV. All remnant of the sun was finally gone now, and the darkness laid over everything. In the blackness we both pulled out our phones and stared into the blue luminous light. The caller who refused to quit was Billy. It was out of character for him to call that many times. I didn't bother with the messages and just called him back.

As it rang, I drove the SUV out of there.

"Grimes, damn it. I've been trying to call you."

"Yeah, I was tied up," I said. I could hear Jinky giggle.

"Well fuck," Billy lit a cigarette and breathed it through the phone. "That was some smoking hot ride you got there. I fixed it up for you though." Billy kept with the vague communication. We knew what we were talking about, but if there were ever any listeners it would be hard to nail us on specifics.

"Yeah, I got a good deal on it. What do I owe you?"

"Nothing brother. It's all good." Billy's tone was smooth and settled down from the hysteria he had in his voice. It had a calming effect on me too. If he knew things were good, not just between us, and as a whole, I could relax. That's the nature of our partnership, that's putting your life in someone else's hands.

"Good, man. I have one more stop to make, but I want to catch up tonight."

"For sure." Billy hung up.

As I drove along the dark highway towards town, I pictured dropping by Billy's, going down to the cellar and just sprawling out on his grandmother's old couch with a cold beer. It was the safe den of a mother bear. The high stress games we played always ended in laughs and dreams of the next score on that worn out couch. In the meantime, there was nothing to do but lay low and resist spending the stolen cash. The problem this time was, my job wasn't over.

When you case a joint, it's to learn all there is so there are no surprises. You watch for routines, and habits of your mark. When they leave for work or return or when shift changes take place, you take note. It's a lot like dating. You take a girl out learn about her likes and wants, her habits. You do all that so, hopefully, there are no surprises. People are not always predictable. When you think you have them figured out, they surprise you, sometimes in the worst way, like the guard who goes for his gun, or the girl with the secret fetish. The surprises can be exciting as hell, but for a guy like me, I need to know exactly what I'm getting into.

The pieces were finally all out before me, but I couldn't make out the shapes or how they fit together. I needed to know more.

Chapter 13

I had to make a call and bring this to an end. She had yellow hair and a black heart. I ate of her honey and like a killer bee, she stung me to death.

"Hello," her tone was serious and flat.

"Catch you at a bad time?" I said.

"Oh Roger, no, no." Her voice came back perky and high, she wore a smile as she spoke. "So, what's up?"

"You sound like you never expected to hear from me again."

"No, I just, with you, I never know. I like what we have going Roger." She smiled at me through the phone but what once was sweet was now sour.

"Yeah, me too." I said, fighting to keep my voice from shaking as bad as my hand holding the phone. I killed seven men because of her. I had been beat up, tied, stunned, and spit on because of her. Billy would argue I did this to myself because I allowed it, that on some cosmic level I chose this. He was always trying to balance things with the universe. My universe was balanced. I stole but I made the effort to give back. I was never a social justice warrior or anything but gave where needed. Now it was upside down and righting it seemed impossible. I could only accept the way things are and face the reckoning for us all.

"I'd like to see you tonight. First, I'm going to take a nap, I'm beat." I let it hang there for a while. She didn't fill the dead space, so I said, "Well, how about it?"

"Yeah, okay Roger. I'll text you the address, I think you know the place." Her voice was terse, and she hung up.

The text came through. I knew the address alright. I started a fire there, but it hadn't burned all the way yet. It was time to go back and set it ablaze. This time I would make sure it was nothing but ashes.

I was going to bring this all to a close tonight. Willis Sanford was not the straight-shooting lawyer I pegged him for. Everyone has two sides, Sanford, me and now Chloe. She had me alright. I had been used by her and Sanford, a straight up sucker for them both. For a guy trying to keep to himself, I had jumped into bed too quick with these two. They each had their own ideas about me and how to use me. One had to fall tonight for using me.

For now, I wanted to make good on taking that nap. Any nervous energy was drained. I ached and bled from places I didn't know I had. I wanted to sleep and wake up with a new body.

My old burlap couch was a relief on my tired body. I stretched out on and shut my eyes. It didn't last. Someone knocked on the door. *Shit they sent hitmen over fast.*

With the Glock in my hand, I looked through the peep hole in the door. The scrawny figure of Jinky was standing looking back. I waited a few seconds, looking for movement behind him or to the sides of him.

"What?" I asked through the door.

"I'm going with you." Jinky said and jammed his hands in his pockets.

I opened the door. The young pimp brushed past me into the office. He stood a little taller. His arms were back, and his bird chest was out. He had taken a beating his whole life, it's why he preyed on the young and defenseless. He wanted to punch back, and I wasn't going to deny him.

"Where exactly," I said.

He looked at me blank faced. He didn't know what to do with his hands and suddenly he was in the spotlight and had forgotten his lines.

"To get T-bag." Jinky said mustering energy for the fight.

"No, first I'm going to take a nap. I'm tired." My free hand rubbed my eyes and then along the stubble on my chin. "Go up to the third floor. There is an empty office with a couch. They never lock the door. I'll come get you when I'm ready." I opened the office door to usher him out.

"But"

"Go or go home. I don't care much."

Jinky stood and looked around. He huffed but never said a word as he left. As I shut the door, I reminded him third floor.

My head hit the pillow on the couch. It felt like a blonk but it was thirty-two minutes later. I felt rested though my dreams were hurried and chaotic. At some point in the dream, I was carrying around a Rubix cube, but instead of trying to match the colors I was standing in front of a giant peg board, looking for round holes to put it in.

My eyes opened and the dream faded from my mind. I realized I was sweating and still in pain. My nose had turned a deep purple but was not broken. My side hurt and my arm felt like a thousand Charlie horses stampeded over it. After an Irish coffee, I went upstairs and got Jinky. He was sitting, messing on his phone. He looked up at me, "Finally, jeez, my battery is almost dead."

Back in my office I went to my lower file cabinet drawer and pulled out a pair of tactical cargo pants and Under Armor shirt. Below that was my body armor. Under the body armor was a box I seldom open. In the box I looked over my inheritance, a family heirloom, a Colt 1911 Series 70 Mark IV. I had trained countless hours with it since I was a teenager and now it was time to use it for real.

I looked over my shoulder and said, "Go get washed up in the bathroom, end of the hall."

He watched me for a second with my gear then headed out. I proceeded to get dressed. I pulled out two more pistols, both Glock 30's and found holsters for them. This was the least prepared for a job I had ever been, so I overcompensated with firepower.

I was uncomfortable with all the extra weight of the armor and pistols. Billy and I took corporate security training classes out in places like Nevada, Colorado and Montana and trained with pistols in tactical situations in the past. We decided the old adage would be true, keep your friends close and your enemies closer. So, what better to learn their tactics than to train with them?

Jinky walked back into the office, "Holy shit." His mouth was agape. "Damn, Call of Duty. Do I get to play dress up too?"

"No." I said and handed him a compact 9mm. "Here, can you handle this?"

Jinky held it with his palm open. He looked at it and then took it by the grip and held it out. He made a 'pow, pow' sound with animated recoil.

"Just stay behind me," A premonition flashed before my eyes of getting shot in the back with my own pistol. "Actually, stay to the side of me."

****

It was after 11 pm and still in the mid 70's outside as we headed out across the empty parking lot to the SUV I took from the gangbangers. The only other car in the lot was my own pickup. I had a jacket on to cover the hardware I was carrying. I hadn't bothered with dumping the SUV or even changing the plates. I was tired and the extra effort wasn't worth it to me anymore. It wasn't like T-Bag would report it stolen.

"We'll ride separate." As my words slipped out of my mouth, I caught the movement of a dark shadow just off to my left. I went low and hurried for the cover of my truck. Someone from the shadows opened fire. I leveled my own pistol and fired as I moved.

While I was still shooting at the shadowy figure, the squeal of tires ripped over the pops of our small arms fire. An old Pontiac sedan cut through the lot. The man from the shadows stepped out, gaining confidence as his compadre neared. I seized the opportunity and dropped him.

The man took three shots to the chest, my last three. I dropped the magazine and reloaded as my back hit the safe side of the truck.

The Pontiac slowed as it moved past the dead shooter then picked up speed. I stepped out and saw the driver move one hand off the wheel and come up with a pistol. We exchanged a few quick rounds. His bullets hit my truck mine hit the windshield. As he neared, I started to run perpendicular with him and leaped into the open rear passenger window.

The car accelerated and I righted myself. Next, I pointed the barrel down on the base of his neck and fired. He jerked the wheel and hit an island in the parking lot holding twin palm trees. The sudden impact sent me over the driver and through the windshield. I rolled off the hood and onto the pavement.

Jinky came running over, "Holy shit that was rad!"

I was stunned, both, by the impact and my actions. I hadn't thought it through, just acted.

There were bits of glass in my neck and back of my head but otherwise I was in O.K. shape. The three rounds of forty-five I sent through the windshield helped when I crashed the rest of it out with my head. We had to hurry, there was no time to stand around the scene of a shootout.

"Take the SUV." I said and hurried to my bullet ridden truck. The V8 fired up and I peeled out of there.

The pool hall was close, which didn't leave me with much time to think. Planning and plotting were not something I was in the mood for. They know who I am and where I live. Putting this off will only prolong the inevitable death I have accepted is coming. My plan? Just kick in the front door and take as many filthy, complicit, disgusting scum bags with me.

It's a far cry from where I started with this thing. Being a P.I. was supposed to be just like being a thief, hiding in the shadows, going undetected until I got what I came for. Willis Sanford turned that upside down. He picked me out, knowing who I was and what I have done the whole time. I was the perfect candidate to carry out his avenging angel bullshit in an attempt to clean up *his town*. Well, this is my town too. When I kill Milo and end her evil organization, I will pay a visit to Willis. If he wants vengeance, then I will deliver it.

The C-10 was chugging as I pulled off US 1 and onto a poorly lit street. A bullet must have hit something vital, but I didn't have time to check. I swung my C-10 over to the side of the street a block down from the pool hall. Before I got out three sedans with tinted windows pearl colored paint pulled up fast and stopped in a hurry. My hand went to my side iron. There was one Crown Vic on twenties with an aftermarket exhaust to my right, an old Buick with a landau top to my left and an early 80's Lincoln Town Car straight in front.

With the high beams of the Lincoln on me, I lost track of where Jinky parked. They had me, I was caught in the headlights and not moving. Then the high beams flashed. I waited and they flashed again.

Nothing happened. No one else showed and no one got out of the car. I waited.

The tinted window of the Lincoln went down, and smoke bellowed out. I heard a voice call out, "Roger Grimes, get out tha car." A dark hand with gold rings waved me out.

I pulled my forty-five and slipped the barrel end into my right cargo pocket. With my left hand, I reached for the door handle and got out.

I stood with the high beams in my face.

"Kid, don't worry you can put the gun away." The voice said.

It was a familiar voice, not one I expected or wanted to hear but one I could trust. Besides, if it wasn't trustworthy, I'd already be shot to pieces and bleeding out in the cab of my truck by now. I put the forty-five away and showed my palms.

The doors on the Lincoln opened. All I could make out was a long slender silhouette on the driver's side and a larger, more rounded, built man on the passenger side. The men walked closer. I saw a rigid scalp of cornrows, a gold chain, and the outline of a goatee long enough to get a small braid in and I thought I saw the shape of a smile.

"Yo, Roger." The driver said. This time, closer, his voice too sounded familiar.

I nodded to the lean man then the older man stepped into view. He had white hair and that gleaming gold tooth. "Hello kid."

Only Smitty ever called me kid.

"What's up?" I said to both.

"It's me D'marcus."

"From high school?" I said thinking out loud.

He stepped forward and I saw his hand come up to shake. We slapped hands and greeted each other as if we had been friends in high school. We hadn't been.

"Are you here to kill me?" I asked cutting the crap, this wasn't a high school reunion. Why an old mobster like Smitty was hanging out with a 3rd Street gang-banger like D'Marcus was beyond strange.

D 'Marcus snickered, "Nah man." His tone grew somber, "But I ain't here to save you neither."

"No honor among thieves?"

"Shit, you're the only thief here. I sell drugs and pimp hoes."

"Little hoes?"

"Nah, nah, nothing like that. Look man I know what's been going on. Hearing rumors and shit until Smitty here came to me and confirmed it. Delroy been doing shit on the side and using 3rd Street for cover, you know what I'm sayn'?" He leaned back relaxed like on the Lincoln.

I kept quiet. I knew what he was getting at, but I wanted to hear him say it.

"Roge," Smitty jumped into the conversation now, "I called D'Marcus here and told him what you were up to. I think you should hear what he has to say."

I didn't know how or why Smitty was keeping tabs on me. I didn't care. I was on my way to kill more people tonight and these two were delaying it.

"Look here, Delroy my people, my family, but he done messed up." D 'Marcus patted his chest softy as he spoke. "I know you just after that white bitch for what she done, and they gonna go down with her."

"I'm gonna kill them all." I said with ice on it.

D 'Marcus stood straight, his arms falling to his sides, "You do what you need to. I'm just saying it ain't a 3rd Street problem no more. We cut Delroy loose, he on his own." D'Marcus put out his hand again. We shook and I walked back to my truck.

As I grabbed the handle to the door Smitty called out, "Hey kid, you got friends." He probably had a smile on his face, but the headlights were on and I only saw an outline of an old man.

They pulled out slower than they pulled in, this time letting the bass thump as they left.

Smitty stuck his neck out for me. I wanted to know why, but there was more to my night to come. D 'Marcus's little visit took a lot of tension out of me. It subdued a fear that my fight wouldn't end today, that tomorrow, the bullseye on my back would grow. Tonight, I could end this if I lived. I should have told him thank you for that.

Chapter 14

Night had fallen and the fight was here. Above the doors were the faded green and red neon lights spelling out Pool Hall. I'm easy going until I'm not. Tonight, I buried that and relied on my stubborn streak to carry me through this. I had the training and the fortitude to win. I looked at Jinky next to me, shaking and ready to cry. His cycle of violence would end here, just beyond those faded lights.

I met up with Jinky a block away and we walked to the pool hall together. The kid walked a little straighter, his hand was in his pocket, griping the pistol. Every few steps he would jerk it to the top of his pocket and then let it slide back down.

I wished it was Billy there by my side, but I owned this one. There was no way I could ask him to come back into this and besides the less he knew about tonight the better he would be for it. In a way, I did choose this job. I took it on separate from Billy and his mentoring advice, determined to do something on my own. Things had gone south, but after tonight I hoped to right them.

We stood at the curb looking at the three storefronts of the small strip mall. A large fluorescent light hummed with electricity as it beamed down covering the small parking lot in a blue-white hue. I performed a weapons check. I looked at Jinky. He was staring straight at the door to the pool hall.

"This is going to hurt," I said.

"I'm going to make Milo hurt." Jinky's lip was curled as he spoke through gritted teeth.

"Channel that hate and it will carry you through this."

Jinky nodded. He reached into his pocket and felt the polymer grip of the 9mm. It was time to settle up.

"Are you going to kill me when this over Grimes?" His eyes never lost sight of the pool hall doors.

I looked down on the little man who had lured and trapped young girls into a life they surely did not want.

"If you live through this, Jinky, I won't have to."

We crossed the parking lot. I pushed the door open.

Inside multicolored lights spun, and the music thumped. The bar was charred black and there were black marks along the tiled ceiling. My focus was on the dirty looks and angry eyes of the five people I kept waiting. Their ugly faces craved death. They had committed the worst crimes among society, they hurt little kids. Willis Sanford judged them and here I am to carry out the sentence.

There to my left were Delroy, T-bag and the guy in the long red t-shirt I beat up last time I was here. This time he wore a tight black shirt. The rest of the crew was gone, either scared or went back into the good graces of D'Marcus and 3rd Street. A couple others were lying dead in my office parking lot.

She sat to my right, with her blond ponytail, tight Lycra yoga pants and thin jacket with the zipper down halfway exposing well-rounded store-bought cleavage. The only thing missing from her outfit was the pink yoga mat. What was pink was the handle on her Ruger pistol. To Chloe's left was a white guy, with a hard wrinkled face and cold eyes, and white hair, probably one of Uri's men. His shoulders were rounded, and he had large, veined hands resting on the table.

"Roger," she shouted over the music, "don't tell me you want us to end this way?" She stood up from the small round table she shared with the bulldog looking *Boris* type.

Delroy chimed in on the evil banter, "Yeah, I told you, I'd get you bitch mutha fucka." He smiled. In his waistband was a nickel plated semi-automatic.

Chloe looked to Delroy then to me, "Roger, tell me who hired you and then walk away." She held tight to a purple gripped Ruger, probably a nine-millimeter.

"What! Nah he ain't walking." Delroy chattered as his face was smeared in red and blue lights. Boris stood up and threw his angry bulldog face at Delroy, silencing him with his deadly eyes. Delroy leaned back even further than he was and mumbled some words to make himself feel masculine again after the visual castration.

I labored to breathe through my busted nose and my bruised ribs, the car crash did nothing to help the beating I took earlier.

"In the picture I was given, you were about twelve and went by Milo." I shouted back. She looked at me with large fiery eyes that smoothed out into a slanted pot smoker's grin.

"When did you figure it out Grimes?" Milo asked.

"I was sent to find a girl who ran away. What I found was the woman who killed her."

Chloe's claws came out. She charged forward, I remained still. Her fake press on nails came within inches of my face. "That girl was killed but not by me, you arrogant dick." She grabbed her crotch, "Just 'cause you got one of these means you can do what you want, right? You can just dip in whomever you like and that's that. Well fuck you, Grimes."

She let out a cackle then said, "So dear old dad sent you after me. He duped you into thinking you were chasing a thirteen-year-old girl and for him, I guess you were."

Chloe turned her back on me and walked away. Then she spun to face me again, "Did he tell you how he made this monster, how I was passed around their *poker* parties? Did he?" she shouted.

There it was, *trapped*, the cycle and the damage done that spread like a virus had infected so many. Jinky had been caught in it, and so had she.

"It wasn't just me; they were all doing it. No child left behind; no child was safe." She held the pistol over her stomach like she was going to vomit. The disease was rotting her insides. There never was nor ever will be *normal* love for her. The way I held her, touched her, she didn't feel that. Her responses were faked, timed reactions to make me believe she was alive inside. Sometimes to kill the disease you must kill the patient.

She turned her attention to the other man in the room, "Jinky, what are you doing here? You won't last two minutes out on the street without me. Especially if this shit unwinds. You'll be passed around in prison like, well like the good ole' days of your childhood too." She laughed at his sudden tears. He began to squint and pinch the tears from the corners of his eyes.

Jinky stopped shaking. The tears were evaporated by the intense heat of his hate. He no longer cared about social media, texting, or the skating rink. Freedom was welling up inside and he wanted retribution for himself and the girls he led astray.

The bass stopped, the music was off, and the room was still as we all stared each other down waiting for the move that would ignite this powder keg and bring the whole thing crashing in on us. Somewhere during Chloe's insight into her psyche, Jinky slipped the 9 mm out. No one noticed as all eyes had been trained on me and my hands. He leveled it. In the moments before firing, no one moved, they all saw what he was doing but no one moved. Then the gun went off and everyone scattered, crossing paths as they took cover. I slung lead, belching fire from my forty-five as other rounds screamed my way. It was chaos that put to music would have been a beautiful ballet.

The room filled with smoke and cries for mercy penetrated ringing ears. When I was done with the eight rounds allotted in the magazine, the man in the tight black t-shirt was dead and T-bag was on the floor scrambling for cover leaving a trail of blood.

From around the corner a man appeared with an MP5 and spouted off a dozen rounds of 9mm. I switched pistols to my Glock 30 and quickly laid down thirteen rounds of covering fire that got me to the other side of the bar and got him dead.

I took a dive behind the bar and found most of the broken glass from when I shot Luther. Some wild shots overhead brought additional glass raining down, but it was limited. I swapped magazines in both pistols and returned fire.

Some more screams and the door opened. Delroy wasn't sticking around to finish his fight. I fired a lucky shot that hit him in the shoulder blade, helping push him out the door. I turned and shot T-Bag dead. That was the last of the gun fire.

I came out from behind the bar to see both Chloe and Jinky on the floor. I glanced out the door and saw Delroy sprawled in the parking lot, not moving. The smell of a potato boiled in a gym sock filled my nose. There was no time to figure out the smell when two large white arms clamped down over my arms, forcing the pistol down but not out of my hands.

When the Russian's head smashed into mine, I dropped the pistol. I used the leverage of being taller to my advantage and leaned forward forcing the Russian on his tip toes. Before he could counterbalance, I pushed up and back. I fell on top of him, stale breath whispered past my ears. His breath was gone but his grip remained tight.

I struggled against the locked arms. He was stronger. He rocked us to the right and my hand was trapped under my thigh. His left leg swung around over mine. He was going to try and make a move. I felt the knife clipped inside my right pocket. I began to rock and roll, with every pitch and yaw I gained momentum. He countered, holding tighter. I wiggled the knife out and flipped the blade open. Holding the handle upside down, I nearly slit my own wrist as I gently sunk the blade into the Russian's wrist.

He groaned, sweat mixed with blood as he struggled to maintain his grip. I could feel his blood pressure drop as his grip weakened. I kept jabbing at his wrist. He broke his hold with a shout and pushed off me.

I spun quickly to see the white Russian turn a pasty grey. Blood dribbled from between his tightly held fingers around his wrist wound. He began to circle me, I turned with him. We began to dance with one of us dying in the end.

The Russian grunted and growled as he jabbed and faked getting me to flinch and duck. On his next move, I countered fast and stuck the blade between his ribs and pushed out slinging the blood and flesh from his side. He staggered back on his heels. His pale blue shirt began to run a deep purple. His hand disappeared under the shirt and came out red. The man's head swung and looked at the dead bodies in the pool hall. I watched his eyes give up. It was over for him, unfortunately running was not the option he chose. I had to kill him.

His wild swing left him open, and the knife plunged into his neck. He lasted a few seconds on his feet then fell to die in a puddle of his own blood.

The pool hall fell into the silence of death. A haze of powder collected around the neon lights. I heard a scraping sound and found Jinky.

Jinky had propped himself up on one elbow and had the pistol pointed at her, pulling the trigger, trying to make the gun go off.

Chloe was flopping on the floor, coughing blood, and struggling to get up only to slip on her own plasma. I reloaded my Colt and stood a few feet away. I fired twice, effectively ending her struggles.

Jinky had righted himself in a chair. He was holding his stomach. He giggled, saying, "What'd you do that for Grimes?"

I stood next to him. "Jinky, you don't need to add killing a person to the list of wrongs you've done in your life."

His smiled faded as blood ran from the corner of his mouth, "What makes your wrongs so different?" The blood seeped from between the fingers he used to hold his guts in with.

"Because I have time for redemption."

Jinky fought to get out a second giggle, "I'm gonna Tweet that shit." He took a bloody hand and reached into his pocket for his phone but never withdrew it. He died sitting up in the chair.

My foot caught between the curb and the parking stop taking me down as I staggered out of the pool hall doing my best to hold the fresh blood in. A sticky wet stain formed where a bullet ripped through my pants just below the belt taking a pinch of muscle from the upper part of my glute. There was glass in my left forearm and some in each knee from the bar dive making each step sting with a dozen stabs. The blood loss was more than I thought, more than I had ever experienced. My head was light, with eyes unable to focus. Somewhere up above drops of water began to fall. Each one exploded on my face at impact. I looked up as more began to fall. Soon I could no longer distinguish between the wetness of my blood and the rain coming down. I crawled to my truck.

I sat in my truck trying to stop my own bleeding. Turns out I got winged once in the arm too, the vest stopped one in my chest, reigniting the fire in my ribs. That wound on top of my ass made sitting a problem. I needed stiches but my night was not over. That beer in Billy's basement would have to wait.

A bloody thumb smeared across the black screen of my phone. Pellets of rain tapped a chaotic tune on the metal roof of my truck as I listened on the line for a familiar voice.

"Whatcha got for me?" Willis's voice was upbeat, like he picked a horse and knew it finished in the money and was just waiting on his payout.

"I found her."

"Good, good. You come see me now it's over." Willis hung up fast. He didn't want to hear what I had to say any more than I wanted to tell him.

Chapter 15

I just wanted it over.

I stood outside the CBR building looking up at the light from Willis Sanford's seventh floor office. Through the glass front doors, I could see a security guard at a desk watching monitors, probably TV, but also the monitors. The way I was, bleeding and carrying guns, I couldn't just go in. The security guard would make an excellent witness for the prosecution one day. I had to find another way in.

I went back to my truck and grabbed a small canvas tool bag with my essential B&E tools. When I became a P.I. I figured they might come in handy again one day.

The back door had a simple security keypad. I hooked a scanner up to it and the code break did its thing as it ran all possible combination. The door buzzed and the electronic lock popped. I was in.

The hallway was long with bare walls and concrete floor. There was a camera at the end of the hall above another door with a sign marked "Stairs". On the wall just next to me was a keyed light switch. A couple of lock picks shut the lights off. I moved.

The door to the stairs was open, no cameras. I made my accent to the seventh floor.

Willis sat at his desk and sipped his Remy Martin and champagne. He was unaffected by my appearance. "So, few people have the kind of work ethic you do Grimes. I picked you as the type that would see a job through." He tipped his glass back and drained it. Then he put it down and looked me over.

"I assume you didn't get through the front door like that otherwise I'll need to have a word with security about their best practices." His brown eyes creased at the corners as he smiled.

"Like you said, I came to finish this and that means I won't be on your strings." I didn't pull my pistol, I didn't move at all except for the blood dripping from my wounds, soaking into his thick gold carpeting.

Willis was smart, smart enough to have a contingency plan, smart enough to outsmart me. Once I committed to drawing that weapon it may be the last thing I do. As I waited for his master plan to unfold, I heard a toilet flush.

From a wood paneled wall, a door opened. I drew and readied to fire until I saw a familiar face, a face I was waiting to see in the cellar of his house drinking beer. He stammered when he saw I had drawn my pistol.

"Well shit Grimes, lucky I already pissed, or Willis would have a stain on his carpet." Billy half smiled, like half his face was happy old Billy and the other was worried with anticipation.

I put the pistol down, but not away. "I think we all need to take a seat." I waited until Billy was seated across from Willis. I sat down as well.

The only noise in the room came from Willis who was tapping his fingers against his empty glass. Finally, he stood up. "I'm pouring us another round."

He went to his wet bar and poured himself the usual drink and us, he poured bourbon. He came back and handed us our drinks.

The bourbon went down smooth, it came from a high-end bottle, something I never heard of, but I liked it. The top of my ass burned where I was shot and every time I moved my right arm, the embedded glass wiggled, cutting a little deeper. When I opened my mouth to drink, the bruises on my face from T-bag reminded me how fresh they were. The bourbon eased my pain, so I drank some more.

All three of us sat looking one to the other, a Mexican Standoff except I was the only one holding a gun. The only shots would come from their mouth, and no one wanted to fire first.

Willis was not one for silence, enjoying the sound of his own voice he said, "Grimes, I have deposited your usual and I have," He paused, his hand was up hovering over the backside of the desk near the top drawer, "Shall I?" he asked, eyebrows raised.

I nodded. Willis reached down, slid back the drawer, and pulled out stacks of cash. Seven stacks wrapped in paper bands labeled $5,000.

"This," he said pushing the stacks across the desk, "You do as you like with it."

"I can't take the cash; I didn't complete the job."

Willis's eyes grew large. I could feel Billy get tense.

"Well, I think you did, Hines thinks you did." Willis began to breathe. As he did his shoulders relaxed and his eyes shrunk to normal.

"I killed her Sanford. The Milo girl, Chloe Hines, is dead."

If Willis had a backup plan, he hadn't implemented it yet. He had his courtroom face on, cold and still. Billy avoided eye contact, just staring off, glancing over, but not looking.

"I burned it to the ground, just as you asked."

"Well, you saw what she was into. That spreadsheet you sent me, it has names, Grimes, high and mighty names. Took some decoding on my part and with Monique's help we got them. Tonight, is just the start." Willis said lightly.

Delroy was into something bigger than dealing drugs. 3rd Street didn't want any part of it, D'Marcus knew if they got involved, he'd be submitting to a higher syndicate. That wasn't my concern now. I needed to know how my best friend and I were tied into all of this hell.

"Now I want to know why?"

"For the kids."

"No, damn it. Why me?" I was at the edge of my seat and my bullet wounds continued to bleed.

Willis looked over to Billy who was holding his knee from bouncing. I had never seen my friend and partner in crime so nervous, not in all the heists we had committed. In the minute we had been in this office together, I built a wall between us. Chloe already showed her other face, the scarred side, and the one filled with hate. The hate she couldn't contain was spread to others leaving scars of their own. Willis and her father hired me to stop it.

"Grimes," Billy turned to me, sucked back the whiskey then continued, "I didn't have a choice man."

There were a million nuggets of old Billy's wisdom I could have thrown right back in his face, but I had my own hate boiling. The money sitting before me could never fill the holes in my life now. I grew up, matured, and realized my life as a criminal would be short unless I changed. Unless I found hope. Pope tried to show me that. He had lost his and, in the fall, I lost the little hope I had gained. I was blind to any open door, there was no way out of this.

"Listen to me." Billy continued, "The IRS was breathing down my back, I was being audited for the second year in a row man, they knew something was up. The shop, my own finances, they even checked in on my girl. They got me Grimes, those filthy government revenuers had me. So, I hired Sanford, and he got them off my back. But to do so I spilled my guts to him." Billy was on the edge of his seat explaining why and where he had betrayed our trust. He hung his head, "When it was over, I owed him."

Billy stopped talking. He raised his head to Sanford who said nothing.

The blood from my wounds continued to soak into my clothes. The chair I sat in was ruined forever.

I looked at Billy, "What did he want Billy, I know you couldn't pay so what did you trade for?"

Billy swallowed hard, looked at Sanford then to me, "You brother. He wanted you."

To pull my weapon and squeeze off two rounds would be admitting I lost the tiniest piece left in me that wasn't yet trapped. I knew killing my best friend and mentor would bury me even deeper than I was now and what little piece of hope I clung to would be lost forever.

Sanford said softly, "He did it to protect you, Grimes. *It* would have got back to you." He sat up and sipped his drink then went on to say, "You did it Grimes, you destroyed that whole sex ring. You burned it all to the ground and saved countless children tonight." Willis stood up. His mouth parted with a small smile, unsure if it was welcomed. "The cops are involved now; they've taken several of the girls in. Tonight, you set them free."

I thought of Joss and her sense of being trapped and of Chloe and how she never would let herself try to get out of the trap. Pope had tried, he tried with me, and he tried for himself. Maybe he didn't make it in the end but that doesn't mean I could not.

Willis continued, "See Grimes, this wasn't about you. Gregg Hines is a friend of mine. Since I've known him, he has suffered from a deep, dark depression. He called me up one night, out of the blue, and told me he had cancer and he needed to confess a few things. I told him there was only one way to absolve them. I introduced him to Roger Grimes. And you did not let me down son." Willis had his hands spread wide like he was ready for me to hike him a football. I didn't like being used, but I understood now why he did it.

"Oh, I should have told you, let you in on the full story. I've known some of these players for some time, ate with them at the same charity events, played golf, lots of other things the rich do around here, except that one thing. I think they all knew where I stood. Now we have names, thanks to you. We can finish what we started. That house of cards is coming down now. All the way up to the state capital I hear. There are all kinds of officials implicated in this. It's amazing, just amazing." He had a smile on his face, his eyes were bright like watching a shuttle launch down at the Cape.

I popped up with my pistol level taking away the glow in his eyes. My adrenaline was rushing through my veins making it hard to keep my sight clear and my hand steady. The pistol was straight on target for Willis's head.

The lawyer leaned back in his chair with enlarged eyes behind square steel eyeglass frames. A single dribble of sweat cascaded down his wrinkled face. As I vacillated to end the puppet master's life, his eyes became slits as he sat up in his large leather chair. Leaning forward, his hands spread on the desk, he cleared his throat.

"Son, you weren't just picked through random circumstance like your friend here tells it." He hummed like agreeing with a sermon in a crowded church. "I've had my eye on you for some time. You weren't nothing but a pickpocket and a car thief, just gutta trash. You got locked up, tossed through the revolving door of our prison system. But you came out different didn't you. You broke something in there, but it wasn't your spirit. See that town out there, the one on the beach? It needs breaking and as good as the cops might be, they can't do what you can do, they can't go where you can go. With your P.I. badge and my standing in the legal system, we have a chance to make a difference!

"A long-time coming Grimes, a long time coming for the wrong doers down there!" Willis had risen to his feet, he stood with his chest out and arms raised like a preacher in the pulpit. The barrel pointed at him had descended. The whiskey dulled my pain and slowed my reactions, but my mind was free to wander, instead dug a little deeper. Searching my feelings, I knew it wasn't in me to kill him.

I knew then that killing Willis would be a certain death sentence by the state. He had files on me going way back and all of that would come out. There was no defense argument here, not for a thief turned murderer. The door slammed shut on my cage, but there was still one last thing to complete.

I turned and went for the door leaving the cash on the table.

"Wait the money," Willis said.

I held the door, "You can pay me when it's over."

Willis's hands fell together, and the smile was gone. He knew where I was going.

Chapter 16

Rest would only come in the moments I forgot to look over my shoulder.

I drove along the river heading north on the peninsula. My C10 that I spent so much time and money with Billy customizing was overheating, and I could put my fingers through the bullet holes in my door. There was a loud clacking coming from the motor and I had lost oil pressure. Like my truck I was beat and feeling woozy and had trouble keeping my head level on my shoulders.

The houses got bigger as I went. I turned off the road and found the front gate open. The drive was brick, lit on both sides by small solar powered lawn lights. All the windows shown black in the three-story Key West style house. The roof was a red tin and the walls a pale yellow. There was plenty of tropical vegetation covering the walk up to the front door.

I got through the front door easily enough. Inside the house was bigger than it looked from the road. In the entranceway I had a choice of two curved staircases inviting me up. Beyond that was the formal living room. It was dark but in the living room, through the large glass windows I could see the river and the lights twinkling from the mainland.

I crept on. I went on to my left, through a kitchen larger than most restaurants. Passing through I saw a light on further ahead past the dining room with a table for fourteen, easy.

The family room was cozy with an overstuffed dark brown leather sofa and love seat. A standing lamp with a low watt bulb cast warm golden light through the room. The walls were wood paneling and there were photos of Gregg Hines with top state politicians, the ones you see in the news making flowery speeches with big ideas of how to spend the peoples' money.

Behind the couch was a custom-made wooden bar that was heavy on resin. Above the bar were the Yale University glasses and more photos with politicians that now run their own world charities. Gregg had taken part in global initiatives, to stop capital punishment and banning guns by taking money from corrupt governments that murdered dissidents in the streets. So, I guess he was a real swell guy getting rich fighting for human rights.

Seated in the leather love seat was the long, lanky frame of Gregg Hines. His eyes were red and glassy and the skin around them raw and pink. He had not shaved in days and wore a green sweatshirt with a couple of old bleach stains dotting it. His jeans were faded, and he had on slippers over his feet. And there was a revolver in his hand.

"Willis said you weren't principled, that you were smart but no morals. He said if she talked, explained everything, you wouldn't come for me." Gregg's voice was slow from the half bottle of bourbon he had sucked down. With his free hand he reached out to the small end table and poured bourbon into a glass. He sipped.

"It wasn't until I met with you, I knew different. I knew you would come. I looked into your eyes and realized you wouldn't let me get away with what I have done." He looked down into his glass and then finished what he had poured.

I had hardly spoken a word to him and damn near forgot about him. I didn't see in myself what he had seen, but he was right. Being a thief, you can't have morals, from the beginning you know it's wrong, you know you hurt people even if insurance covers their loss. It's great to read a book or watch a movie and the hero is a thief or contract killer with his own moral code, like somehow deciding your own morals makes you the good guy. Well, that's bullshit. If you want to be a criminal check your morals at the door, because you're going to hurt people. The only thing you can have is loyalty and even that is fallible.

"I guess it's for the best. If they don't get me the cancer will." Hines studied his bourbon like a fortune teller looking into a crystal ball trying to see the future. Peering into the weary eyes of an old man who destroyed so many lives including his own daughter's, I stood ready to take his life, not for justice or retribution, there is no higher court here. Because to claim I am justified, I would have to admit there is justice and I can't do that, not yet. But I have hope for that day. This man's life would end tonight the last one to break the cycle.

I made my move, but he moved first. His revolver came up quicker than I could clear my holster. I felt my breath catch in my throat. My eyes zeroed on the round barrel pointing at me. Then he turned the pistol on himself and fired.

His skull broke apart and brain matter scattered, covering most of the lampshade, toppling it over with force. The bulb shattered and the room went dark.

It was over.

The End

Thank you for reading the first installment of Grimes and his crusade to clean up his hometown. I hope you have enjoyed his journey so far. Grimes' Retribution A Debt Paid in Full is out now and ready for you to keep reading! Please leave a review and if you liked it, tell a friend.

-H.A.L. Wagner